ROtten
Little
animals

KEVIN SHAMEL

Eraserhead Press
Portland, OR

ERASERHEAD PRESS
205 NE BRYANT
PORTLAND, OR 97211

WWW.ERASERHEADPRESS.COM

ISBN: 1-933929-91-X

Copyright © 2009, 2011 by Kevin Shamel
Cover art copyright © 2011 by Lars Maria Maly

This book is dedicated to Audrey.

We share imaginations.

To Terri for her love and support

and for always believing in me.

And to Julio. He was a good rat.

CHAPTER ONE
Cat Fight

Scaredy Cat crashed through the fence, snapping off the tops of three pickets. He twisted in the air and sailed behind the pointed projectiles into the backyard. Rain began to fall. Scaredy landed in the grass, hunching his back and hissing at the striped cat bouncing toward him from across the yard.

The other cat—Stripey—launched himself into the air and Scaredy leapt straight up to meet him. They clashed two feet above the grass. Scaredy bit into Stripey's neck and dug at his belly with one hind foot.

Stripey blocked the gut-scratch and bit Scaredy's left foreleg.

The cats crashed to the ground.

The fucking meat truck drove into the shot again.

"Cut! Cut! Fucking cut the fucking shot!" Stinkin' Rat screamed from under a large hydrangea plant.

Scaredy helped Stripey up. "Let's get out of the rain," he suggested.

They skittered to the hydrangea.

The camera chickens converged with the director/producer on the replay monitor.

Stinkin' Rat said, "Aw, it's fuckin' great, cats, fuckin' great. Stripey, that's the best leap of the morning." The rat sat rapt, his little black eyes picking out every detail of every second of video. "Nice moves, both of you." He shouted, "Great work with the collapsing pickets, rats!"

Stinkin' watched the fight on the monitor, three

camera views on split-screen—one tight, one medium and a wide shot. After a moment he said, "And the rain came down... And then that fucking Iowa Meats truck drives past for the third fucking time!"

He reached up and grabbed a branch from the bush and started shaking it. Rain fell on the gathered animals. The camera chickens spread wings over the monitor. Two of them shit on the damp ground at their feet.

"I mean, what the fuck is with those idiots?!" The rat stopped shaking the branch. "Julio, did you get those assholes on the phone?"

Stinkin's son appeared from behind the hydrangea stalk. "I got 'em Dad. They said they couldn't find the bus stop."

"Did you tell them it's right beside the fucking backyard they keep driving past?! Where they're wrecking my fucking shot?! Did you tell them that not only are they late, but they're turning my fucking *on location* shot into something that looks like it was filmed in front of a fucking green screen?! Did you tell them they're ruining my fucking movie?!" The rat stood on his hind legs and shit. Pellets piled at his feet, and he stepped to the side.

Julio cringed and said, "Uh, no Dad." He pointed to the bus stop behind them, where just over the picket fence, two men unloaded a meat truck. "You know, uh, they're *human.*"

Stinkin' kicked a rock at Julio. "I know that. I didn't mean... I wasn't—Great Gaia!" He turned to the gathered actors and crew. "All right, once these assholes unload the guts and stuff, we're filming. Until then, take a break."

The rat waved everyone away and yelled, "Dirty Bird!"

Animals wandered the backyard.

A Steller's Jay—much like a Blue Jay, but with a black head and no white spots—swept down from the top of a giant cedar.

6

"Yeah, boss?" he asked upon landing.

"Break time. Where's your flask?"

The bird produced a silver flask from under his wing.

The rat drank from it and handed it back to the bird.

"Thanks, Dirty."

"No problem, boss. I'm gonna go have a smoke." The jay jumped into the air. "Hold onto that, I'll be right back."

Stinkin' raised the flask and took another pull from it. "Julio!"

The young rat joined his father and they strolled along the inside of the fence under the bushes.

"So you and the boys get those guts into the yard. Once you're set up, we're going to do the ending of the fight scene and the zombie-cats. We'll need some shots of the yard with guts, so we can edit them into the whole fight. Fucking meat men. How're the zombie-cats?"

"They're in the shed." Julio nodded to six rats lining the picket fence. "Boys," he acknowledged.

The rats nodded silent greetings and went back to watching the men unload the meat truck.

"They get the money?" asked Stinkin' Rat. He drank from the flask.

"They got it," answered one of the rats. He pointed to an envelope sticking out of the back pocket of a meat man.

Stinkin' and Julio walked on, Stinkin' Rat telling his production assistant/set director/stunt coordinator/son how he could assist him.

The rain poured and tapered off. The rats strategically distributed guts, bones, and hide across the backyard.

The chickens set up their cameras.

Julio manned the marker.

Stripey and Scaredy had practiced their carefully choreographed fight scene during their break, foregoing

7

munching on the sparse catering laid out under a derelict picnic table in the corner of the backyard. Scaredy was outfitted with blood packs.

Stinkin' Rat sat just under the hydrangea.

It began to rain again.

Dirty Bird perched in the tree above them, on the lookout for interloping humans. He gave the all-clear tweet.

When the actors were set on their marks and the cameras were ready, Stinkin' Rat said, "Roll cameras."

Julio slipped in front of the shot and snapped the marker. "Scene seventeen, take one."

Stinkin' Rat yelled, "Action!"

The cats leapt into the air, grappling with each other. They fell onto the patchy grass—rolling and scratching, screaming, spitting and slamming each other into mud. The chickens panned according to Stinkin's filming sketch and frantic paw-signals.

Scaredy grabbed Stripey's neck, pulling his gnashing teeth away from his face. He said, "I'm. Not. A. Zombie!" And tossed Stripey backward.

Stripey lunged back at Scaredy, swiping at him with abnormally long claws.

Julio cued the wind machine.

Rain flew sideways into the fighting cats.

The chickens zoomed in on Stripey's face. Later they'd edit in zombie-Stripey close-ups.

Stripey swung toward the camera, raising long, bloody claws. "Braaaaainnnns," he drawled.

He lunged at Scaredy Cat and slashed the blood bags taped to Scaredy's chest. Fake blood splashed in wide gouts; a stream sprayed perfectly across one of the cameras' lenses.

Scaredy staggered backward toward the piles of guts, clutching at his abdomen, squeezing blood in geysers between the pads of his paws. "No!"

8

Stripey howled.

Scaredy fell.

"Cut!" shouted Stinkin' Rat. "Print that shit! Fuckin' gorgeous!"

The cats joined one another, smiling congratulations with fake-blood-covered faces. The chickens secured their cameras and clucked excitedly. The rats swarmed the actors.

Itsy, the vagabond Yorkie, turned off the wind machine. He glanced across the street.

"Holy shit!" he yelled.

He barked and barked while congratulations played out in the middle of the yard between actors and crew. Finally, Stinkin' Rat took note and followed Itsy's pointing.

Across the street, in a second floor window of a big old house, a young boy sat watching them with binoculars.

"What the fuck?!" screamed Stinkin'.

The animals stood frozen in the yard, staring up at the boy across the street. The rain stopped falling. Every chicken pooped.

"We're toast," said Scaredy.

"Act natural," said Julio.

"Dirty Bird!" screamed Stinkin' Rat.

Dirty bird flew to join the gang in the yard. "Yeah, boss?" he chirped.

Stinkin' slapped the jay across the beak. "You flighty fuck! Look at the kid with the binoculars across the street staring right the fuck at us!"

The bird turned and looked across the street.

The boy sat staring straight at them.

"Oh. Him?" The jay hooked a wing that way. "He's nothin'. He's watchin' the chick that lives in the house behind us, over there." He hooked his other wing the other way. "No worries." Then he fell over.

The animals helped Dirty Bird to his feet and slapped off some mud from his feathers.

9

Itsy shouted, "He's gone!"

Everyone looked across to the window and saw that it was indeed lacking a binoculared child.

"Shit!" yelled Stinkin'.

Dirty Bird said, "He's jus' checkin' out the girl. Look." He pointed again.

The bird staggered to the far fence and hopped upon it, urging the director to follow. Stinkin' Rat joined him. Dirty waved his wing toward the house across the yard. There was a nude woman visible through her window, lying on a big fluffy white bed, her legs spread, masturbating furiously with a humming pink vibrator.

"See?" asked the inebriated jay.

"Yeah," drooled the rat, "I see. Get a chicken over here with a camera. Tell everyone else to take a break. And no more vodka for you."

* * *

The kid was not watching the masturbating woman. Courtney. He *had* been. He watched her almost every Saturday morning. Courtney was like cartoons, only lots more bonerish. But the cat fight had caught his attention. He swung away from the porn window and zoomed in on the yard where the cats were fighting.

At first it just seemed like an awesome cat fight.

But then the kid saw a rat sitting under a hydrangea in a director's chair. He saw a Yorkie working a fan—no, a wind-machine! And two—three!—chickens operating cameras. And other rats running around. And guts in the grass.

When the kid noticed blood packs on the cat and that the other cat had weird, fake, too-long claws on one paw, and when he saw the end of the fight with all the fake blood and cheesy acting, he began to freak out a little.

10

Then the scene was over. The rat was on his feet. The chickens were messing with their cameras.

The kid watched the animals gather in the yard, patting each other on their backs. The rats were—high-fiving?—the cats. The chickens left their cameras and were clucking around. A rat helped remove the blood packs. The kid began to really freak out.

Then the dog with the wind-machine started barking. He was staring right up at the window.

All the animals gathered and stared at the kid. A Steller's Jay flew from the cedar to join them.

The boy wondered what was going on.

The rat chittered at the bird.

The bird did a lurching dance and fell over into a mud puddle. All the animals rushed to help it up. The kid ran down the stairs while they weren't looking.

CHAPTER TWO
What is it With Rats and Humans?

The cats leaned against the high fence, sharing a joint, while the rat and a chicken with a wing-held camera perched above them and filmed the human fucking herself.

Scaredy asked, "What is it with rats and humans?"

"I don't know, but it's sick. Pigs also like people." Stripey looked around. "Dogs, too, for that matter."

"I know. It's so gross."

"They're all so gross."

"Ew, they are. Pigs, rats, dogs and people. Ew. And don't get me started on *wild* animals."

"Double ew. Ship 'em all off to a yucky planet somewhere else."

"Exactly."

"Mmhm."

"This is good weed."

"It is. I stole it from that dick kid I live with. Mixed it with some nip from the yard."

"Sweet. I love your nip."

"It's the shit. Fo sho. Remember when that asshole Roger used to piss on it? Ick."

"Oh, I hate to say it, but I was so happy when Roger got hit by that car."

Stripey laughed, blowing smoke in dragon puffs. "You don't hate to say it."

From the top of the fence, Stinkin' Rat stage-whispered, "Shut your faggy feline fuck-holes before I make

12

you play zombie-cat anal-rape victims. And give me the rest of that joint, you fuckin' sissies."

Stripey handed the joint up to the rat, and the cats slunk away without a word, like cats do.

Stinkin' Rat went back to watching the chick with the giant tits stick things up her huge human pussy. He drank vodka and smoked the doobie. His rat cock grew stiff. He couldn't help but sigh contentedly, even as rain began to pour again. Even as he saw Dirty Bird slip around behind the shed full of extras. Not even that fuckin' jay could wreck the moment. He raised the bird's flask to his retreating blue ass and took a long gurgly pull.

Dirty Bird was just trying to get away from everyone. He could have flown, but he was pretty drunk, and he'd eaten half a Xanax, and he just needed to sit down and have a smoke.

He hopped around behind the meowling shed of zombie-cats and collapsed against the wall. He pulled a smoke from his wing-pouch and lit up. Exhaling, he let his head fall to the side and closed his eyes. The rain pattered through some raspberry vines and fell on him in a green mist.

Dirty finally felt decent. He sat and smoked, feeling better with each drag.

Until a huge shadow passed over him and stopped—chilling the mist clinging to his feathers.

He opened his eyes.

A human was staring at him. The boy from the window. His face was a wing away.

"Fucking shit, kid!" The Steller's Jay shot purple and white poop onto the gravel, splattering his feet and feathers. He dropped his cigarette and fluttered against the thorny vines. "You scared the crap out of me!"

The boy staggered backward, away from the swearing, smoking bird tangled up in raspberry vines, smearing his wrinkly bird feet in a pile of his purple-swirled poop. The boy couldn't believe what he was seeing. Most especially what he was hearing.

He pointed at the struggling jay.

Once Dirty Bird freed himself from the raspberry poop trap, he hopped toward the back-stepping kid, cooing, "It's okay. It's okay, kid. No big deal. I'm a talkin' bird. No big deal."

The kid backed away toward the garage. Dirty Bird began to panic.

"Kid! It's okay! Don't fuckin' worry! I'm not going to hurt you!"

"You. You're a blue. A blue." The boy backed away slowly, keeping his eyes on the bird.

Dirty hopped toward him. "Shh! Be quiet! I'm just a trained bird. A, uh… A circus bird. From the circus. I'm from the circus. Come on, kid, calm down. Just calm the fuck down."

The boy started to moan.

"Shut up, kid! Stop that noise." He flapped at the boy.

The little human stumbled backward, eyes on the bird. He continued moaning.

"Aw, Dirty Bird, you fuckin' retard!" came Stinkin' Rat's voice from behind the jay. "It's that kid. You fuckin' idiot bird!"

The kid squealed and pointed at the rat. He stumbled and fell on his ass, crab-crawling backward. The rat and bird advanced.

The bird was yelling, "It's okay!"

The rat was swearing and yelling into a cell phone.

The boy made it to his feet. He turned and lurched toward the garage. He looked over his shoulder just in time to see an angry pink blur run him down. He fell to the gravelly driveway with two hundred and sixteen pounds of hog on his back. He lost consciousness upon impact.

"What the hell, Filthy?!" squawked the jay, swooping over to the pile of person and pig.

Filthy Pig bounced once on the little human, cracking his back. He looked sideways at the bird. "What? Stinkin'

14

told me to."

"Where did you come from?" asked Dirty Bird.

"I was sleepin' in the van. Stinkin' called me."

The rat joined them. "Is it dead?"

Dirty Bird got close to the kid's face. His sour human breath stirred the dust at the bird's shitty feet.

"He's alive," the jay said.

"Want me to kill it?" asked Filthy Pig, gathering himself for a good bounce.

"Let me think," said Stinkin'.

Julio approached his father. "Dad, we can't kill him. We should call the police. Or we should get out of here and let him wake up thinking it was his little boy imagination. Of course, we'll lose this location…"

Stinkin' Rat looked over his son's shoulders to the gathering animals. The crew of rats shuffled around looking nonchalant as always. Two of the chickens were filming the situation. The other chicken was still on the fence capturing Stinkin's new side project. Scaredy and Stripey were holding each other, staring at the pig atop the boy. Itsy looked hungry. The zombie-cat extras crowded in the shed's doorway. They looked gross and scared.

Itsy said, "Could take months to get a new location."

Stinkin' Rat spun around and called to Filthy Pig, "Off it, Pig. Julio's right. We can't kill it."

The zombie-cats sighed together.

Stinkin' said, "But I'm not losing the day's shoot *or* this location. Tie the kid up and gag it. Put it in the van. We'll worry about it once we're done filming."

Julio screeched, "What?!"

Stinkin' ranted, "It took six weeks of casing this place. The owners only leave for this long one day a week. This day. I'm not losing this location. This is the perfect backyard! And what about the guts? What about the shitty fucking catering? What about per diem for this ridiculously huge crew?! No. We put the kid in the van and we think about it later. Right now we shoot my fucking movie. Get those extras calmed the fuck down and on the set. Now!" He turned back to the pig. "Get that kid in the van, Pig."

Julio walked off shaking his head.

Filthy Pig, Itsy and the rats got to work wrangling the unconscious human into their windowless child-molester van.

Scaredy and Stripey bounded to the backyard.

Stinkin' Rat stalked into the backyard, leaving a trail of pellet-turds as he walked.

They filmed the zombie-cat blood and guts scenes while Dirty Bird sat in the tall cedar and whined to himself about his dumb luck. He didn't see the lady walking her poodles stop right below him and stare at the zombie-cats tearing up guts in her neighbor's backyard, and the zoo-crew filming it.

But he did shit on her—stinking fear and vodka bird shit—and since the lady was heavily medicated and thoroughly disgusted, she staggered off vomiting on her dogs (who had to pretend like *they* didn't know what the fuck was going on) and forgot the whole thing about the zombie-cats and camera-chickens.

They stopped shooting for the day half an hour before the homeowner was due back.

"I want all the zombie-cat extras to come back to the studio!" shouted Stinkin'.

The kid was conscious when the film crew crowded into their van with the zombie-cats.

He screamed behind the duct tape plastered across his mouth. Filthy Pig raised a hammy hoof, and the boy stopped screaming. His eyes went wide.

"Get us out of here," said Stinkin' Rat.

Filthy Pig donned his flannel shirt and stocking cap. The pig played human and steered 'n' geared with a handicapped conversion kit.

They drove to their hideout.

CHAPTER THREE
The Inspiration Strikes Back

"Of course we can kill it. It's all we *can* do. It's what we have to do." Stinkin' Rat paced the plush carpet in his office. "Shit, Filthy'll kill the kid *and* eat it. Right, Pig?"

Filthy squealed his leprous laughter.

Julio twitched his nose.

Stinkin' said, "Aw, come on, I'd have a nibble. Don't tell me you don't like human, Julio."

"It's not that I don't *like* human. I just choose not to eat it. I certainly don't choose to be a party to murder. Even if it is a human boy."

Filthy Pig laughed harder.

Stripey snickered, and Scaredy looked at him as if he were shocked, though he wasn't at all, because he'd certainly shared a homo-flavored snack with his feline friend. More than once.

Stinkin' put his paw on Julio's shoulder. "Well, regardless of your tastes, we have to kill that boy. It's the law. It saw way too much. Fuckin' Dirty Bird *said* way too much. But what's done is done. We eat it."

Julio shook his father off. "I'm not eating any of that kid. And the law says we turn him over to the authorities, not that we kill him ourselves."

"But that involves paperwork. And again, cops on the scene. That means we'll be shut down. Filming will halt. It's so much easier to just eat the little fucker. Everybody does it."

"I don't think anyone should eat that kid," Itsy piped up from the doorway.

Stinkin' Rat narrowed his tiny marble eyes. "Why do you say that, Itsy? You seem to be the hungriest of us all." The rat smiled a yellow smile.

Filthy Pig snorted.

Itsy laughed a short doggish laugh. "Oh, I'm hungry, all right. But not for little boy. My cravings are for much more than the tender flesh of a young man-thing."

The Yorkie jumped up on a chair. He said, "I've been thinking since we nabbed that kid. Thinking about a screenplay. A story about a bunch of animals that kidnap a human. I know it's been done. But it's never been done with a human kid acting the part of the kidnapped human. And I have ideas for a script already. Something edgy and realistic. Maybe about a *film crew* that kidnaps a kid." Itsy's big brown eyes widened. He stared down at Stinkin'.

"Shh. Let me think." Stinkin' stood looking at Itsy for a long, quiet moment.

The room was silent.

The cats reclined in the corner. Itsy stood watching Stinkin' Rat. Julio implored his father with his eyes. Filthy Pig farted silently. The only tell was his flaring nostrils.

"I fucking love it!" the director/producer/kidnapper exclaimed.

"What?" asked Julio as if he'd just been wakened from a dream.

"Boss?" asked Scaredy.

The rat said, "It'll make us completely fucking legendary! Itsy, my boy, you're my writer. Bang that shit out, and let's make a movie!"

Julio looked from Itsy to his father. "Dad, are you serious? Are you thinking at all? Do you realize what that would entail? We can't ask the kid to act in our movie. It's *illegal*."

The elder rat smiled wickedly down at his son. "We don't have to *ask* the kid to act. We kidnapped it." He poked his son in the chest. "And since when have you worried about what's legal and what's not?"

Julio waved his paws. "It's the only real crime there is! We'll be put to death! We're already fucked, as far as we've come with this. We should have left him unconscious on location. No human would have believed him, even if he'd been dumb enough to tell anyone about an English speaking animal film crew—a, a, smoking bird and a foul-mouthed rat! Or we should have had him taken care of legally. But we put him in the van. And he's still in there! We have to figure out what to do with him so he won't talk, and it's not put him on the payroll. He's a *human*!"

Itsy said, "It's either that or kill him. Like you said, he's a human. It's the law."

Julio narrowed his eyes at Itsy.

Stinkin' told the room, "Look, Itsy's right. We either have to kill the kid or make a deal with it. We'll tell it the whole score—secret animal society, underground cinema, everything. We'll tell it that we want to make a movie with it, and that if it goes along with us and keeps our secret, we'll let it go.

"And we'll tell every other animal that the kid is a fucking robot that Itsy, our genius FX dog, came up with. We'll say that we destroyed it after filming so that no one could steal it. Or that it caught on fire or walked off down the street, bumping into baby strollers and asking for a dollar or some shit. It'll work. Otherwise we blow a chance at something huge. And kill the boy."

Julio said, "I don't like it, Dad. If we get caught, we're dead. And it's not up to us to kill the child."

Filthy Pig said, "We'll need everyone sworn to secrecy. Even the clucking chickens."

Stinkin' rat smiled a nasty smile. "Oh, no problem

with that, Pig. You're all under contract—everyone."

Itsy said, "This will work."

The cats stared at each other.

Stinkin' Rat said, "Julio, get the whole crew in here."

* * *

After a few hours of discussion, misinterpretation of animal-law, reminders about contracts, some name calling and general abuse—everyone's favorite being when Filthy Pig said to Dirty Bird, "Get a fucking sphincter, bird."— the animals determined that they would indeed make a film about a film crew kidnapping a human child, with the human child they'd kidnapped playing the part of the kidnapped child.

Everyone wanted a raise. The zombie-cat extras all wanted parts in the kidnapping movie and individual credits in the original zombie film when it was finished. Stripey and Scaredy wanted a month more vacation time per year added to their contracts. Dirty Bird wanted more vodka. Everyone told him to shut up.

Stinkin' called a meeting with Itsy to start on the script. He sent the rats to get some food and announced that there would be a production meeting in an hour or two.

It fell upon Julio to approach the human. Scaredy and Stripey went with him to the van.

The van was parked in what functioned as the crew's garage—once three rooms in the basement of a burned-down church on the outskirts of town. Most humans didn't know the tangle of trees and vines had ever been a building. The ones who explored never knew about the basement. Because it was hidden. Which meant it was dark. And no one had left on a light in the garage.

Scaredy Cat flipped on the lights. The van started rocking.

Stripey opened the back door of the van. It creaked

loudly, echoing in the wide room.

Julio hopped inside.

The boy shrieked and scooted to the front. The van smelled like pee.

"Oh, yuck," said Scaredy, arriving at the back door.

"I *know*," said Stripey.

"It's okay, kid." Julio stepped further into the shadows toward the boy.

The kid started kicking.

Julio dove out of the way. He shit as he rolled, and little beads of rat poop bumped across the bare floor of the van.

"Hey!" yelled Stripey, leaping into the van and onto the boy's heaving chest. He sunk his claws in deep until the kid was shrieking spit from the sides of the tape across his mouth. "Stop kicking!"

The boy stopped kicking.

The cat took his claws out of the boy's skin. "That's better. Now listen to Julio. And don't you move."

The rat approached the boy. "I'm going to take the tape off your mouth. Please don't scream. It won't matter if you do, no one will hear you but us. And it will only bother us. Nod if you agree to keep quiet."

The kid's eyes grew wider than they already were. He nodded vigorously.

Julio ripped off the tape.

The kid yelled, "Help! Help!"

"Calm down," said Julio. He tore at the tape binding the boy's wrists.

"You're a rat! You can't talk!"

"Calm down. It's okay." Julio freed his hands.

The boy passed out. He came around quickly. Tears streamed down the little human's freckled cheeks. "What's happening?"

Julio removed the tape from the boy's ankles. He asked over his shoulder, "Scaredy, could you get the kid

21

something to drink?"

The cat nodded and took off.

The boy rubbed his wrists, glaring at Julio and Stripey.

The rat moved to the open door of the van. "Come on over and sit on the bumper. Scaredy'll be back with something to drink." He patted the corrugated floor.

The kid shuffled to the door and kicked his feet over the bumper. "What's happening?" He peered into the lighted room.

Stripey slipped past and dropped to the floor.

Julio looked up at the kid and asked, "What's your name?"

The boy looked down at the rat. "Cage."

"Well that's a shitty name," quipped the cat.

Julio said, "Well, Cage. I'm Julio. This is Stripey."

Cage nodded, wiping tears from his eyes.

Scaredy Cat came into the room pushing a cart with a mug and carafe on it.

"Here ya go, kid," Scaredy announced. He dropped to all fours and let the cart roll into Cage's knees.

"Ouch!" Cage righted the carafe and poured brown liquid into the mug.

Everyone watched him take a sip.

"What is it?" asked Julio.

"Cold coffee," answered Scaredy.

Cage drank down a mug. He spit grounds from the tip of his tongue and poured another cup.

"There was no water?" Stripey asked.

Scaredy shrugged.

"How can you talk?" Cage stared at the cats.

"Well, we open up our little mouths and words come right out. How do *you* talk, human child?" Stripey sashayed in a circle, purring girl-style.

Julio said, "All animals can speak."

Cage looked around at the animals. "No you can't. Your brains are too small."

Stripey jumped onto the boy's lap, knocking away the cup of cold coffee. He put his face up to Cage's. "It's not the size of your brain, it's how much of it you use. Asshole."

"What do you mean we can't?" asked Julio. "We're talking to you right now."

The kid leaned backward, trying to get away from the leering cat. Stripey rode him down to the floor of the van. "I hit my head. This isn't real. I'm hallucinating."

"What do you know about hallucinating?" asked Scaredy Cat, joining his friends in the van. "How old are you, anyway?"

"I'm twelve. I watch TV, that's what I know about hallucinating."

Stripey jumped off the kid's chest, digging his claws in for launching. He and Scaredy hopped out of the van.

"Ow!" Cage sat up. "Anyway, you animals might really be here, or you might not. You definitely can't talk. I'm going to leave now." He slid to the floor.

Stripey climbed the boy's jeans and t-shirt. He dug his claws into the kid's abdomen.

Cage screamed and flailed at the cat. Stripey scrambled onto the boy's back. He gripped a hunk of scalp, hooked his rear claws into the hollows of the kid's collarbone, and put a paw across one of his eyes—flexing his little needle-nails into tender eyelid skin to make his point. Cage stopped flailing.

"Just sit down!" yelled Julio.

Cage sat on the floor, in the puddle of coffee.

Stripey let go of the boy, whispering into his ear, "How's that for real?" He jumped off him.

Scaredy said, "Just be cool, Cage."

The boy rubbed at the bleeding claw-pricks on his head and shoulders.

Julio stood in the back of the van. He said, "Cage, we've got a problem. You see, animals *can* talk. It's the biggest secret in the world. We stopped talking to humans a very long time ago. So long ago that you all forgot we could. We did that on purpose. We want you to think we're dumb. It's a trick we're playing on you.

"See, if a human finds out that we speak, if they find out that we drive vans, and make movies, and steal humans' drugs, and trade in bestiality, and basically do countless things in the world that any human does not know we do, we usually kill that human."

The boy tensed—eyes widening.

"If that's what we were going to do to you, Cage, you'd be dead already. Relax. You see, we *all* have a problem. All of us." Julio began to pace along the edge of the van. "You may or may not have noticed that we are a film crew. You stumbled onto our shooting location."

"That bird!" Cage looked from animal to animal, remembering his neighbor's backyard. Remembering the chickens with cameras and the smoking bird.

"Yes. Dirty Bird. He was a little drunk. Anyway, it's the *law* that we call the cops if a human finds out that we can talk. It's THE law. We don't have any other laws, really. Law of the Jungle, I guess. That and, 'Never ever ever, no matter fucking what, let a human know about any of this shit I just told you about'. That's basically it. For breaking that law, animals get death."

The rat stopped and stared at the boy. "Get what I'm sayin'?"

Cage shook his head no.

"We broke the law. You're alive."

Cage sat for a minute and thought. Finally he shrugged.

Julio looked to the cats. They shook their heads.

Julio said, "We want to make a movie, Cage. With

you as the star. We want to make a movie about us kidnapping you. And when we're done, we'll let you go. But you have to promise to never tell anyone—no humans, and especially no animals.

"You can't tell a single person that you had anything to do with the movie. You can't tell them that animals talk, or where you were for however long it takes us to shoot the film... If an animal finds out about this, they'll have you killed. And if they find out we didn't call the cops on you, we'll be killed. You have to swear to secrecy. That will keep all of us alive. My dad, the crew boss, says he'll kill you if you don't agree. And he will, Cage. He will."

"Then he'll eat you," added Stripey.

Julio glared at Stripey.

Cage grimaced. "You want to make a movie with me in it?"

Julio nodded.

The cats, flanking Cage, nodded.

"Yes. We want to make a movie where you play a kidnapped kid. And we're the kidnappers."

"But I'm not really kidnapped?"

Julio looked at Cage's big brown eyes. He looked to the cats. They shrugged.

"Nope. You're not really kidnapped. You're an actor, that's all."

"Okay," Cage said. "Can I get something to eat?"

CHAPTER FOUR
Stinkin's Big Stinkin'
Production Meeting

Cage was led into the room, seated at a very low table and served an old warm Coke. He waved around the table at the assorted animals. They sat on cushioned stools. Cage sat on the rug. He still thought he might wake up, or that the animals might all disappear. Or at least they'd stop talking. But the rat introduced him.

"Okay. Everyone, this is Cage. Cage, this is everyone. You'll get their names later. Everybody welcome our new actor." Stinkin' nearly managed to say the word, *actor* without smirking.

Cage jumped when Filthy Pig snorted loudly at his introduction.

Dirty Bird raised his head from inside a martini glass. "Hiya, kid." He pooped over the edge of the table.

Rats murmured. Chickens tittered and shit on the floor. The actor cats ignored everyone and dug into a bowl of tuna liver.

Itsy said, "Pleased to meet you, Cage."

The gang of zombie-cats stared from the corner. Some ate from buckets filled with something raw and bloody.

"Have some food, Cage." Stinkin' waved his paw at the table.

Cage picked up an ear of corn.

"Not my corn!" screamed Filthy Pig from across the table.

The boy dropped the corn.

Julio handed him an apple. "Here, kid."

Stinkin' climbed atop a drafting bench near his chair at the head of the table. He cleared his throat and let the chatter subside.

"All right, everyone, we're at work. Itsy's writin' the script. He's got a few scenes done already, and I like it. Basically, as far as the filming schedule goes, we're already filming." He motioned to cameras planted around the room.

Animals looked around, commenting on the cameras and the angles and the fact that some of them had noticed that they were on, and some hadn't. The chickens, having set up the room, clucked loudest.

Stinkin' continued, "We're going at this from a *reality* angle. Hidden cameras, shaky-wing camera action. Itsy's got this great idea for *human-view* angles and such. But what that means is, we'd like to keep everyone in character as much as possible." He surveyed the table.

Cage was grabbing food and stuffing it into his mouth.

The animals began to chatter.

Scaredy asked, "What does that mean? Like, from *now*? But none of us has seen a word of the script. Are we on the clock?"

Stinkin' smiled. "Be yourselves. We're making a movie about a *film crew* who kidnaps a *human boy*." He let their realizations occur.

The animals grew quiet in thought. They all turned to Cage.

"What?" the human asked.

Dirty Bird slurred, "You gotta play the victim, kid. Twenty-four-seven." He fell over on the table.

"I gotta what?"

Filthy Pig flew over the table and head-butted the kid back into unconsciousness.

Itsy and Filthy Pig dragged Cage across the room and propped him against an old bag of golf clubs in the corner opposite the zombie-cats. They began taping him up again.

"What's going on, Dad?" Julio stood on his hind legs and narrowed his eyes.

Stinkin' said to the room, "We're not lettin' the kid go." There were murmurs. "Itsy, Pig and I were talkin', and doing that is just ridiculous. He'd tell." A few rat droppings rolled down the slanted table and caught on the pen-tray, adding themselves to a ragged row of rat turds of varying ages.

"But I just told him we'd let him go! We can't kill him now." Julio scampered onto the table beside his father.

Some of the chickens nodded.

"Of course we can. We can and we will. It's the law. Sort of. Anyway, we can't ever let him go—you all know that. If we did, we'd all be fucked. Our film would be fucked. We can't afford that. This opportunity is gold! And it fell right into our paws. I've got plans for this movie. *Big* plans. We're gonna make this *more* than a reality film. We're going to make it a fictomentary—the meat of cinema, full-on fodder! Close to a documentary, but with enough creative license to make the fuckin' thing interesting.

"I'm tellin' ya, Itsy and me got this worked out. It's gonna be fucking brilliant! The kid will look so real that it will always be a mystery. With him dead, no one can ever prove he was a real boy. Let them try! It will add to our fame.

"We'll be the most famous animals of all time. Lassie? That no-talent bitch will be forgotten. And I don't mean that human TV bullshit she did. I mean the real stuff. This will be bigger than any of her underground Frisbee free-for-all films. Bigger than her and Mr. Ed's six–hour porno.

"This is history-making. We can't afford to have the kid found out. Let's say he doesn't tell a single human about being kidnapped by talking animals filming a movie. What if an animal saw him later?" Heads began to nod. "No. He dies. And for now, we kidnapped him. No need to act about that. We treat him like a kid we napped. Got it? We'll go over character sketches and the basic outline after dinner. Any more arguments? Legitimate fucking questions?" Stinkin' looked around the room.

Cage moaned through his nose as the pig and dog finished taping him up.

"You can't be serious." Julio shook his head at his father.

"Oh, I'm serious. And you'd better be serious, too." Stinkin' Rat poked his son in the chest. He turned to the room, "You'd better all be serious. We're not fuckin' around about this. This is more than life or death."

Filthy Pig snorted.

Itsy snorted.

Julio skittered down the drafting table. He stalked out of the room without a word.

The animals watched him go and turned back to Stinkin'.

"He'll come around." He met the eyes of the crew, surveying their convictions. "Everybody in?"

There were affirmatives. Not even the chickens hesitated.

"Good," said the rat. "Itsy will hand out what he's got written so far—mostly character sketches and a rough opening. Then we'll eat and get down to business."

Itsy handed out scripts.

CHAPTER FIVE
Julio Tells a Secret

Cage awoke to darkness and the overwhelming stench of feces. He pushed himself to his hands and knees and vomited. His hands slipped in something slick and sticky. He fell into his puke and puked again.

Cage heard movement above and behind him—scratching.

"Hello?" He turned around.

A loud plopping sound directly in front of him caused the boy to jump backward. He slipped in the puddle of vomit and fell into a large, soft pile of what he easily identified as the source of the stench.

Whoever was above him could no longer maintain composure and burst out laughing. The animal—it sounded like a dog—ran away and the laughter grew dim.

The room began to brighten as Cage became accustomed to the darkness.

Just as he realized where he was, a light came on from high above.

Cringing, he peered between his dripping fingers. He stood in the center of a small room filled with animal waste. Animals looked down on him through a grate in the ceiling. As he looked up, three rats pointed their asses at him, lifted their tails, and dumped their little bombs at Cage.

There was much laughter. There were cameras and lights, and a microphone was lowered between the grates.

Stinkin' Rat yelled, "Hey there, Cage! Welcome to

your new room!"

The animals started hooting and screeching. They laughed and slapped each other on the backs, pointing down at the boy and howling.

Cage screamed, "What are you doing to me?!"

The rat shushed the animal racket. He looked around at all the animals gathered around the boy at the bottom of the pit.

He brought his paws to his foamy muzzle and shouted down at Cage, "We're shitting on ya, boy!" He turned and shat.

The other rats in the crew let loose. Stripey shit on the kid. Itsy peed on him, having been the one to shit in the dark just before.

Cage fell to the floor with his arms over his head. He dry-heaved.

Crap fell on him.

Stinkin' Rat yelled down, "Have fun with your roommate!"

The animals left. Most were laughing crazy animal laughter. The lights snapped off behind them. All but the twinkling spotlight from a camera fixed to the grate.

Not long after the animals went away, a door opened in front of Cage and light flooded his horrible room. When he saw the silhouette in the doorway, he realized who'd been missing from the shitting party above him. The pig.

Filthy Pig stood for a moment, watching the boy grow afraid.

Then he said, "Welcome to my room."

Cage slipped backward to the far wall, knocking his shit-covered head against the cold, wet bricks of the sub-basement animal toilet. He sobbed.

Filthy came in, locking and closing the door behind him.

He snuffed over to the boy, tossing feces with his

31

snout off the ragged paths that crisscrossed the room. Filthy took the crying, shaking lump of boy in his teeth and dragged him away from the wall.

"Don't worry," said the pig to the boy, "I'll give ya something to cry about."

* * *

Stinkin' Rat reclined in his little rat bed in front a giant flat screen TV, watching his gold-edition DVD of *Fucking a MILF Like I'd Like To Fuck a MILF*. He had his ugly rat dick in his paw and was just about to come when his sissy kid barged in.

"Oh, gross, Dad! Aw, damnit—it's humans, too. Ick, Dad. Ugh." Julio shielded his eyes.

Stinkin' ignored the little whiner and kept rubbing, while on the screen a cock bigger than his whole body slid into a glorious woman pussy. He came while Julio searched for the remote and finally ended the cacophony of human sex that blared through the producer/director/human-porn freak's bedroom.

"Mmmmm….aaaaaahhhhhhhhrrrrrrrrrrrraaahhhhh! What the fuck do you want, Julio?"

"I want you to stop jerking-off to humans."

"Shut up." Stinkin' lit a smoke.

"I don't think this is smart, Dad. I think we're going to get caught. I think we should kill the kid right now. But we shouldn't make a movie about it."

"What are you talking about, Julio? I thought you loved humans. I thought you wanted to let the kid go." Stinkin' mocked his son with a sappy-sick mimic, "He won't think it was real. He won't tell." He blew smoke at Julio's face.

Julio coughed. "Stop it, Dad. I'm serious. No one is going to believe that Cage is a robot. Or FX of any kind.

He'll look so real because he *is* so real! Someone's going to find out. It's him or us."

Stinkin' turned on the news. "No one's going to find out. And we *are* going to kill him. When we're done with him."

"This movie is bad news."

"It isn't, Son. It's the best idea I've ever had."

"You didn't have the idea. Itsy did."

"Well, fine then, it's the best idea I've ever stolen. Now get out of here. I need some sleep. So do you. We have to go over the script tomorrow."

"You think he'll have something by then?"

"Ah, hell, the dog's practically got it written. He's wanted to write this for years, so he says." He took a drag, dropped his cigarette and crushed it on the floor with a calloused hind paw.

"I don't like Itsy."

"Oh yeah? Well, I sure do." Stinkin' motioned toward the door. "Now go to sleep. At least, get the fuck out of here."

Julio stood still. He flared his eyes at Stinkin'. "You know, snuff films are nothing new."

Stinkin' Rat laughed and clapped his claws around his son's shoulder. "Snuff film? We're not making a snuff film. We're making a fictomentary. And we're not killing him in the movie. In the movie he turns into a pig and lives happily ever after."

"Wha—?" Julio let himself get spun around toward the exit.

"Yup. It's all about transformation and dehumanizing the beast within—it all ends fine for the kid. Then we kill him. I told you, fantasy and reality all combined. It's fabulous, my boy, fabulous. You'll see. Not only will we get away with it, but it will make us untouchable. Now go get some fuckin' rest." He shoved his assistant toward the door.

"Uh, okay," Julio conceded. He left.

Stinkin' watched him go.

He turned the TV back to whole-rat-sized cocks pounding whole-rat-sized pussies and masturbated until he passed out with his little dick in his paw.

Dirty Bird found him like that in the morning. He took a series of photos before he woke the rat.

* * *

Dirty accompanied Stinkin' to the breakfast production meeting and script run-through.

"Itsy," said Stinkin' Rat, settling down at the table, "whatcha got for us?"

Itsy dropped a fat stack of papers in front of Stinkin'. "Got it all."

There were murmurs. Especially among the rats, all of whom were amateur screenplay writers.

Stinkin' flipped through the pages to the end.

Julio was reading his copy and sipping at his coffee. "It ends just like you said it did, Dad. The kid turns into a pig, and everyone loves him. Wouldn't it be great if that really happened? Seems the whole movie is about torturing the kid until he turns into a pig. How would that happen? Why would a film crew want to *do* that? Why do *you* want to do that? Do you think he's going to turn into a pig when you're all done filming? I don't think so. I think you're going to kill him and eat him instead."

"So fucking what?" asked Itsy. "Yes, we're going to kill him. *You* want to kill him. You thought we should call the cops when we first found him. You've wanted him dead all along. We're not only prolonging his life, we're immortalizing him! And yes, then we're eating him." Itsy turned away laughing.

The chickens clucked. The cats snickered. The

zombie-cats moaned.

Julio asked Scaredy to take his copy of the screenplay. He sipped at his coffee and stood. "I'll be in my room," he announced. He left without looking back.

Stinkin' watched Julio leave. He frowned. "Where's Pig?"

"Sleepin' in, I guess," said Dirty Bird.

"He had a long night," said Itsy.

"Ew," said Scaredy Cat.

Stripey put a paw on Scaredy's hind leg and nodded.

"All right," said Stinkin', "I'll talk to Pig later. Julio, too. Here's what I want you to know—this is one of the two production meetings we'll have. You take your scripts and shooting schedule and work out whatever parts you have that involve one another. I'll meet with you individually to go over details if need be.

"Chickens, you've got shot calendars and scene sketches, but you won't really have much to do but check memory and batteries and run the control room. We've got two cams set up on the kid—one attached to his head, and one on the room. We'll do the scenes without the kid on a different schedule. I'll hand that out at our next meeting. The kid's scenes will be shot by then.

"For now, study your scenes, be yourselves, and be sure you show up on time. I'm not sure how long this kid's gonna last, so we're gonna stick tight to the schedule. Any questions, come find me or Julio."

"What the hell is with my character?" asked Scaredy as the animals began to get up. "Am I playing some sort of bestiality freak?"

Itsy nodded slightly to Stinkin'.

Stinkin' said, "You're playin' a human-lover, yes."

"Ew. Talk about creative license."

Stripey said, "You can do it. Just pretend you're at home."

"Zing! None for you tonight," Scaredy clawed the air at Stripey and gave a, "Reeowrrr."

One of the rats said, "Two weeks? You think we can shoot this in two weeks?"

Stinkin' snapped his attention to the rat, but when he spoke it was to the whole room. "We *will* shoot this in two weeks, or *less*. We will. There are no sets save for this production studio. Most of us live here. There's no commute. We're filming all the time. There's really not many of you that act with the kid directly. Most of the work will be editing. We've got the kid's stamina to think about, and I want to get this finished and submitted to Animaux."

There were gasps.

"Really?" Stripey and Scaredy asked together.

"Really," Itsy answered.

Stinkin' nodded and smiled.

The crew-rat smiled, too. "All right, boss. Animaux it is. Always wanted to be involved in an Animaux Festival film."

"Well, now you are," said Stinkin'. "Now you all are. So let's get to work."

The animals grabbed breakfast remains and made their way out of the kitchen just as Filthy Pig barged through the door.

"Better be food left," the pig grumbled on his way into a chair. He scooped up bowls and plates from the table and heaped them in a pile.

Stinkin' watched the crew leave, and then the pig eat.

"Pig, did you feed the boy?"

Filthy didn't look up from his pile of plates. He smacked food. "No."

"Good. Don't. Scaredy's doin' it on camera."

The pig ate. Watching him made even Stinkin' Rat feel ill.

"In fact, don't do anything to the kid from now on unless I know about it."

"Fine." Filthy rooted at the table, knocking two plates off. They shattered.

"Good Gaia, Pig. Get some fucking manners." The rat leapt from his seat at the table and skittered out the door.

Filthy burped, throwing a bone that whipped over Stinkin's head. "Fuck you, rat!"

* * *

"Fuck you, rat." The boy crawled against the wall—away from Julio.

"Come on, Cage. I want to tell you some things."

The boy edged away.

"Cage."

Quietly, Cage said, "I used to *like* animals."

Julio sighed. "Yeah. I'm sure you did. I really don't mind humans." He moved closer to the boy.

Cage stayed still.

"But Cage, I have to tell you. This really has nothing to do with not liking you. Or not liking people. It's about a secret, Cage. The biggest secret we have. You see, we need people. But we need them to think they're special—better than us. We need you for your thumbs. And we need you to believe your thumbs make you better. We need that for all of our futures. So no matter what, people can't learn about who animals really are. Not yet. Not in either of our lifetimes. Even if you'd lived to be an old man."

The boy sat crying in the shitty dark. He listened, but tried not to believe.

"I'm going to tell you the rest of the secret, Cage. Because you have to die. Because you're not going to leave here, no matter what any of them tell you. Don't believe that they'll let you go. They're going to kill you, Cage. They

37

have to. I'm going to tell you why it's important that you die before they kill you, though. Maybe it will help you feel better about all of this. I'm really sorry it had to happen. You seem like a nice enough kid. Do you want to know the future, Cage?"

The boy looked down at the rat. "I want to know what's happening," he whispered.

Julio told the child the secret of the future—a crazy story about thumbs, dinosaurs, and the hidden alphabet. It made even less sense than what was happening to him at the time. Cage felt no more comfortable about his coming demise. In fact, it bothered the boy even more than being killed by a bunch of rotten little animals for no fucking reason at all. Even the insanity that had taken hold after the first night in the pig's toilet room failed to numb the itch inside Cage that told him to survive.

The child just nodded.

Julio said, "I'm leaving, Kid. I'm leaving the fucking country, I think. I'm really sorry about all this. I wish you hadn't looked out that window when you did."

Cage said, "Courtney..."

The rat shook his head. "See ya, Kid."

"I hate rats," Cage whispered.

CHAPTER SIX
The Price of Fame

Stinkin' Rat made his movie. He hired Itsy as Julio's replacement. No one even looked for Julio. Stinkin' said he'd always been a little pussy, and that it was good riddance and all that big-talk that greasy, underground film producing rats say.

Itsy was rarely seen away from the rat after that. Except when *interrogating* the prisoner with Filthy Pig—off camera.

Dirty Bird, who had hoped to be the new production assistant, became the gopher instead.

Cage became nearly feral.

The shooting time extended to three weeks. Itsy made some changes to the end of the script that needed some additional scenes shot.

Stinkin', Itsy and a camera chicken spent five days hidden in and around the yard where they'd abducted Cage. Itsy wanted some shots of the boy's house. And of his parents driving in and out of the driveway. And of them pacing in front of windows. And of police coming and going. And of his mother sobbing.

Two weeks and six days after they began filming, Stinkin' and his crew threw a two day-long wrap party.

On the second morning of the party, the animals let Cage out of the toilet and gave him a bath with three changes of hot, herbed water. They fed him fresh food for breakfast. They bathed him again. No one beat him. He did not even see the pig. They gave him a shower. He let the animals lead him around. He stared straight ahead and shuffled his feet when he walked.

While Cage was in the sauna, Stinkin' addressed the crew from on the table, toppling against one of Dirty Bird's human-sized martinis. "Congratulations, everyone! We're only a week over schedule, and that counts two days of partying!"

The rats, cats, pig and dog cheered. The chickens clucked. Dirty Bird burped. The zombie-cats silently watched Stinkin' with unusual attention and anticipation.

Stinkin' tipped the huge glass and poured the drink on him, managing to slurp some up. He said, "All we have left is editing, a little bit of animation and killing the kid."

More animal cheers echoed around the table.

"It's almost time for the feast! Crank up the tunes!" Stinkin' fell off the table and popped up laughing. He waved his paws.

One of the rats cranked up the tunes.

Stripey and Scaredy began dancing with each other. The other animals clapped and stomped, watching the actors. The chickens began strutting in circles around the pair. The rats began hopping, and Dirty Bird leaned on one foot and then another, shaking his tail-feathers. The zombie-cats milled around in a mob.

Stinkin' danced his way to Itsy and Filthy Pig. He yelled loudly in the pig's ear, "Jus' go pull that kid outta the sauna and break his fuckin' neck. I'm hungry!" He laughed like an idiot, spitting and slapping the pig on the head.

"Really?" squealed the pig.

"Really!" shouted Itsy. "I'll go with ya."

Stinkin' nodded wildly.

Filthy smiled at the dog and the rat. "A round of shots or two first." He snuffled around for a bottle of Jagermeister.

The three drank a few shots of Jager. Stinkin' Rat slid off to dance beside a giggling chicken. He winked to Itsy and Filthy Pig as they went out the door.

Dirty Bird stumble-flew behind them, having seen the wink from his boss and having paid much more attention to what was going on in general than anyone would have suspected.

* * *

Filthy Pig was telling Itsy a joke as they entered the spa. In the center of the room was the toilet grate. They continued past it to the locker room. Neither of them noticed that the two rats who were supposed to be guarding the kid weren't there.

"So the squirrel says, 'Who's nuts *are* those?'!"

Itsy laughed, though it wasn't a funny joke. He could see the steamed-up window of the sauna. He caught a glimpse of something out of the corner of his eye and a whiff of something rotten—just a fraction of a second too late.

Fortunately for Itsy, Filthy Pig was completely oblivious to the ambush that lay waiting. He walked straight into the middle of the locker room, laughing his pig head off while the horde of zombie-cats swarmed him.

"Holy shit!" Itsy batted a patchy black cat away as it came at him with slobbery jaws wide. He backed out of the locker room, snarling.

Behind Itsy, Dirty Bird was tip-toeing through the spa doorway. He froze when he saw the cats jump out of hiding. He squawked and flew back the way he'd come.

The zombie-cats surged over the pig.

Filthy let out a piercing squeal and rose onto his hind hooves. He flung zombie-cats in every direction.

Unfortunately for Itsy, zombie-cats shot toward him as he turned to run. Two of them hit him—one square in the side and the other taking out his hind legs. Itsy tumbled across the floor and bounced over the circular grate in the center of the room. His head smacked into the metal, and he was knocked unconscious. He slipped through the grate and tumbled into the toilet room below.

Cage came out of his sauna-stupor to the most unnatural yowling, hissing, snorting, squealing, howling and spitting sounds ever heard by a human. He looked out the little window and saw the pig covered in cats, and the floor covered in blood and fur.

Filthy Pig charged around the room with eleven zombie-cats sticking to various parts of his massive pig body. A zombie-cat jumped on Filthy's screaming snout. The cat bit into the soft pink part of Filthy's nose and raked its claws across one of the pig's eyes, cutting it open.

Filthy lost his mind. He went screaming around the room and out the spa door with every able zombie-cat not already stuck to him chasing close behind.

Naked Cage stepped out of the sauna in a cloud of steam. Blood covered the walls of the locker room and pooled on the floor. Broken zombie-cats lay scattered about.

It took precious seconds for Cage to realize that he was unguarded and alone. When he did, he ran for the exit. He slipped in blood, hit the floor and slid into the tile wall of the locker room. He broke his left wrist.

Screaming in pain, he stood and backed into the poop-grate. He caught his foot between the bars and fell backward onto the grate, rapping his head on it, tearing his scalp and giving him a concussion. Gingerly, he managed his way off the poop-pit lid and crept out of the spa into the hall.

The pig and the zombie-cats rounded the corner ahead of him and came charging his way. Cage fell back into the spa, landing on his butt and cracking his broken wrist. He yelled as the pig screamed past, still wearing an undead coat of yowling zombie-cats and hotly pursued by the rest of the undead feline gang. They paid the boy no attention.

The boy knew the way out. He'd seen it when they filmed his transformation and liberation scene. When he was sure the pig and zombie-cats were gone, Cage rolled off the floor, peered into the hall to be sure it was clear and ran. He heard Filthy Pig squealing somewhere down the hall as he pushed open the secret door to the animals' production studio.

Cage burst out the door into full sunlight.

* * *

Dirty Bird flew into the party. He swooped over the dancing chickens and rats, screeching for Stinkin' Rat over the Daft Punk song, *Steam Machine.*

He found the rat fucking a chicken under the table.

"Boss!" the bird yelled.

"Get out of here! I'm fucking a chicken!"

"But the zombie-cats!" Dirty couldn't help but watch the rat and chicken go at it.

The chicken's head was pushed into the rug. She was cooing and cawing with each ratty thrust. Her eyes were rolled back in her head. Stinkin' had her wings crossed and pinned behind her with one paw. He was grinning and frothing at his yellow rat mouth. He pulled at her tail-feathers with his free paw. She clucked loudly.

"Oh, uh, Boss. That's, uh… Boss! The zombie-cats! They're killing Filthy Pig and Itsy!"

The rat froze. "What?"

The chicken opened her eyes and looked back at Stinkin'. "Don't stop now," she clucked.

Stinkin' pushed her off.

She squawked.

"What did you say?" Stinkin' demanded.

"The zombie-cats ambushed Itsy and Filthy! They're killing them!"

The rat grabbed Dirty Bird and pulled him along as he ran from under the table. The chicken followed.

"What do you mean the zombie-cats are *killing* Filthy and Itsy?" He pulled the jay through the party. Music blared.

"You know, killing them! Eating them, tearing them apart, zombie shit!"

Stinkin' stopped just outside the dining room where the music wasn't so loud. "Zombie shit? What the fuck?!"

"You know... Zombie-CATS, doing zombie shit like eating brains and shit!"

"They're *real* zombies?!"

"Fuck yes they're real zombies! You told Julio to get you zombie-cats! He got you zombie-cats! Why do you think they just stand around moaning and eating buckets of brains? Why do you think they work for free? What about the zombie-love speech you gave at the martini party last night? Where the fuck have you been?!"

"What?" The rat seemed genuinely confused. "*Real* zombies?"

The chicken poked her head around the corner. "There you are!" she shouted.

"It's not the time," said Stinkin'.

"Boss, we need to—" Dirty Bird was interrupted by a horrifying squeal from down the hall.

The animals turned to see Filthy Pig running straight toward them—zombie-cats riding him down the hall like patchy little jockeys. A posse of undead kitties loped behind.

"Fuck!" screamed Stinkin'. "Why are they doing this?" he asked as he and Dirty Bird turned and ran back into the party.

"You told them last night they could kill the kid!" The bird yelled over the music.

"I did?!"

"Yeah! And you said they could have his brains!"

"I did?!"

"Yeah!" Dirty followed Stinkin' to the stereo.

The rat pulled the plug from the wall, and the party was silenced. He yelled, "What the fuck was I thinking?!"

"You weren't," said Dirty Bird quietly.

The zombie-cat-pig-train crashed through the door.

"Zombies!" Stinkin' shrieked. He held onto the jay. "What do we do?"

"Run!"

"But what about Pig? What about Itsy?!"

Dirty Bird shucked the rat and flew toward the ceiling as the pig careened into the table, scattering zombie-cats throughout the room. The heavy dining room table and its load of booze and desiccated foodstuffs slammed into the wall, dropping two full gallon bottles of very expensive vodka, which shattered on either side of Stinkin', coating him in potato alcohol and blinding him.

The zombie-cats sprang off the floor and furniture and attacked any animal in the room, mewling and droning, "Brains!"

Dirty Bird swooped down and grabbed Stinkin' Rat by the scruff of his neck just as two zombie-cats leapt at him. "Filthy and Itsy are zombies!" he screamed.

"Zombies?!" screamed the rat, wiping vodka from his face.

A chicken head flew past them as Dirty swooned with his heavy rat load. Zombie-cats jumped for them. The headless chicken body staggered across the room, spraying everyone with blood.

"What do we do?!" screamed Stinkin' Rat, his vision coming back so it seemed he was looking through a fish-bowl filled with colorful vomit.

Dirty Bird flapped over to the table. Zombie-cats ran behind him. Filthy Pig, freshly zombified, saw the bird and director/producer/poop-bombardier making their way to the table with a pack of zombie-cats in tow. Filthy slipped and fell in the growing puddle of vodka, wriggled to his zombie hooves and barreled toward the action.

The jay dropped Stinkin' on the table and skittered to a landing. He shouted, "Everyone out of the room!" and grabbed a lit candle from an overturned candelabra. He snatched a napkin from the table and soaked it in a puddle that he hoped was one of his martinis. He touched the candle to it. Blue flames sprang over the napkin as it began to burn.

Scaredy Cat and Stripey jumped up from behind the bar and dashed for the exit, yelping, "Ew! Ew! EW!" as they ran.

Chickens squawked in panic.

The rat crew, those not already out of the room and those not slowly changing into horrid little rat-zombies, made for the door.

Dirty bird handed the burning napkin and the candle to Stinkin' and said, "Don't let these go out!" and dug his dinosaurish bird claws into the rat's little rodent neck. He lifted Stinkin' into the air just as Filthy Pig smashed into the table top, his mean pig teeth snapping at the rat's tail.

Zombie-cats jumped from the table at the swooping duo.

Dirty gained altitude. He flew over the broken bottles of vodka with zombie-cats falling behind him, zombie chickens just coming back to life, and Filthy Pig oinking something nearly intelligible, but mostly just scary, and skittering after them.

"Drop it!" he yelled to Stinkin', who was just starting to understand the bird's plan and burning the fur off his abdomen.

The rat dropped the burning napkin and the not-burning candle.

Dirty Bird banked to the left, avoiding Filthy's last

effort to snatch the rat from him with his piggy mouth. Dirty thought, "Hamtini. No, *flaming* hamtini."

The bird and his rat passenger shot out of the dining room as a pillar of vodka fire erupted behind them.

Dirty Bird yelled, "Close the doors!"

Zombie-cat yowls and an ear-melting zombie-pig screech punctuated the whoosh of the explosion.

The remaining rat crew, the non-zombie-cats and three chickens slammed the doors behind Dirty Bird and Stinkin' Rat as they tumbled across the threshold. A cloud of smoke that smelled sharply of bacon puffed into the hall, and burning zombie-cats thumped against them.

Stripey and Scaredy toppled a bookshelf in front of the doors, just in case the burning zombies figured out a way to open them.

"What the fuck?!" screamed Stinkin' from the floor.

"Zombies," panted Scaredy Cat.

Stinkin' Rat crawled over to Dirty Bird. "Itsy's a zombie? Where is he?"

The bird nodded. "I think so. The cats got him and the kid."

The rat coughed. "The kid's a zombie?!"

Dirty stood and looked toward the smoking doors of the dining room. Feeble thumps came against them now and then. He said, "Yes. The kid is a zombie. The kid and Itsy. We have to kill them."

A stinking Itsy spoke up from behind them, "I'm no fucking zombie."

Everyone yelled, "Yikes!" (Or something like it.)

"Good Gaia, Itsy, you scared the shit out of me!" Stinkin' shouted.

"I see that," answered the dog, nodding at the pile of rat poop under the director/producer/zombie-killer.

Stinkin' moved over and sat down. "Well that sucked."

Burning zombies popped and cracked behind the door.

"We got it on film," offered a chicken.

"No shit?"

"Yes, sir. We were filming the party. The cameras in there are rolling. They're flame-proof. Control room's getting it all."

The rat smiled and smacked his paws together. "I can use that on the zombie film! And I don't have to pay those fuckers!"

"What about the kid?" Itsy asked.

"Dead," said the jay.

"You saw it?" asked the dog. "Where did they get him?"

Dirty nodded and took a step backward.

An explosion tore through the wall behind Itsy, throwing the animals off their feet. Flames, smoke, bricks, drywall, bits of kitchen utensils, meat, vegetables, pieces of the oven and the remainders of Filthy Pig and two zombie cats splattered down the hallway.

While the animals picked themselves out of the rubble, Itsy asked Dirty Bird again about the boy.

"Where did the zombie-cats kill the kid?"

"In the kitchen," said Dirty, pointing through the dust and smoke toward the ruined wall of the burning kitchen.

"We need to put out this fire," said Stripey.

"Itsy, rats, put out the fire!" shouted Stinkin' from under half a spice rack. "Let's clean this shit up and edit a film!"

The surviving chickens clucked half-heartedly.

* * *

The animals finished their film.

They closed off their ruined kitchen and dining room,

after cleaning it up as best they could. They scattered the ashes from the burned-out rooms in the overgrown cemetery behind the crumbled church.

Itsy voiced his concerns that the boy wasn't dead. He said Dirty Bird lied about the kid being done in by zombies in the kitchen. No one paid him much attention. The kid was gone. The movie was done. The past was past.

Stinkin' Rat entered their movie, *A Boy Named Cage*, in the Animaux Film Festival held yearly in France. It won several awards, including audience favorite and best FX, and put Stinkin' Productions into an international spotlight.

With its success at Animaux and subsequent popularity, *A Boy Named Cage* took the remaining crew into instant fame and fortune—it was a groundbreaking and industry-bending film. It was an amazing experience, an emotional rollercoaster, a must-see triumphant adventure of the animal spirit. It was a phenomenon. Everyone wanted to kidnap a kid. Everyone wanted to explore their person side and turn people into pigs. Everyone loved everything about the movie.

The number of knock-offs rivaled any ridiculous human trend. Every animal production company wanted a piece of the human transformation movement. Of course, no one else had a kidnapped kid. Not even the dolphins figured out a decent human automaton. The octopi came up with some terrible CGI.

Stinkin' Productions shone. And made money.

When the Animal Academy Awards came around nine months after the film's release, Stinkin' was packing up his production studio/apartment complex/human torture facility and moving everyone onto a small farm just outside of town.

Only the rat's personal effects—clothes, people porn, unedited footage from the abduction, the original copies of the finished film on various media and some random movie-making equipment—remained in the bomb shelter under the basement. He planned on secretly moving all the footage to an undisclosed location after the Awards.

The Animal Academy Awards, as always, would be held in the crew's hometown of Olympia, Washington in the great Underground Opera House built in 1947 by the Mole Masons and the Animal Academy of Film. Olympia is the birthplace of the animal film industry and center of the growing animal independent film movement.

The Opera House is located directly under Reeves Middle School on the east side of the city. The school didn't open until 1970. It was coincidentally built over the Opera House on land that had been a forest. Because of its location, the awards are held on Sunday evenings to assure the maximum amount of secrecy. Every animal who's any animal attends.

Stinkin' and the crew were up for several awards. Stinkin' Productions was truly big-time. The rat had *made it*. Finally.

CHAPTER SEVEN
Cage Uncaged

Cage ran naked across the rubble of the demolished church. He heard music thumping, and Filthy Pig squealing above it from the open exit. He scrabbled over broken glass and concrete—pulling himself through tightly growing young trees and tripping over vines. He didn't notice that his feet were being cut. He ran.

A bike-riding couple found the bloody nude boy staggering down the center of the highway half an hour later. They gave him some water and short shorts that the female biker had in her pack. They called the police and performed emergency first aid on his broken wrist and bleeding head. They tried to listen to Cage's story, but he spoke disjointedly. When he started talking about being saved by zombie-cats, the girl told him to relax, and he rested his head on her chest.

The police showed up and arrested the couple for kidnapping.

It was all worked out back at the station, as possibly illegal situations usually are. The couple was released and thanked for their part in saving the boy. The girl never got her shorts back.

Cage was taken to the hospital and put under guard. The police interrogated him with the child psychiatrists and hospital clown. The clown's professional opinion after the three-day interview was, "That kid is fucked in the head."

The cops didn't believe a single word of Cage's story

except about the windowless van and that he'd been held in the basement of a church.

They used dogs to track Cage's bloody footprint trail from where the couple had found him. The dogs, being animals, would never have given away the location of any secret animal hideout. Not only that, but they loved Stinkin' Productions films and had been to several parties at the studio. They led the cops to the Krispy Kreme-Starbucks-Drugs and Dirty Money-Hooker Emporium and that ended the trail.

The police gave up on trying to find Cage's abductors. They told the boy to continue visiting the psychiatrist and clown to see if they could pry some information out of him in some sneaky psychiatric or clowniatric way.

Cage was reunited with his parents. They were quite happy to have him home. Cage's father, an avid SUV driving, squirrel-fishing dog-beater, even believed his story. His mother decided to pretend Cage had been at camp, what with all the talk of rats and monkeys and such.

It took Cage six months to recover from his injuries— he'd broken every bone in his wrist several times, suffered a major concussion from literally cracking his skull and tore his feet to shreds by running with glass shards stuck in them. Even after six months, bits of glass worked their way out.

One afternoon, about the time he'd begun to recover, Cage was sitting in his room looking out his window. He never left his house. He rarely looked outside. He never looked across the street at the yard where he'd been taken by the animals. He never watched TV shows or movies with animals in them. When a trial issue of *Ranger Rick* fell through his mail slot one afternoon, he ran screaming into the closet and didn't come out for a day.

Cage was afraid of animals. And rightly so.

It was a rare thing that he sat looking out his window, because birds flew past and cats circled the lawn. He feared he would be discovered.

So that afternoon, while he let the sun shine on his face, he screamed and dove beneath his bed when a Steller's jay landed on the sill under the open window and said, "Hiya, kid!"

Cage came up on the other side of his bed raising a shotgun.

The bird pooped on the sill, jumped into the room and ran.

"It's me! Dirty Bird!" the jay shouted, skittering under the bed.

Cage jumped up on the mattress, pointing the shotgun between his feet. "I'll blow you the fuck away, Blue jay!"

From under the bed, Dirty yelled, "Kid! I saved you! You'd be kibble if it weren't for me! Put the gun down and let's talk!"

"Fuck you!"

Dirty Bird hopped up beside Cage and cocked his head at the boy.

Cage swung the shotgun.

Dirty hopped up on the barrel. He marched toward the boy's face. "I'm serious," he said matter-of-factly.

The boy shook the gun. The bird hung on.

"Cage!" Dirty Bird yelled, stepping up to his boy-face. "Stop it. Don't you think if you were in any sort of danger, that it would be more than me here in the room with you? No one knows you're alive. Only me. I've been watching over you, making sure."

The shotgun wavered. "What?"

The bird said, "It's true. I told them that the zombie-cats got you. I never wanted any of this to happen. Stinkin' and everyone else thinks you're dead. In fact, they're not thinking much about you at all. Other than the fact that you've made them famous and well on their way to being some of the most powerful animals in the industry. The film is the most popular movie ever. But they've been calling you *FX* and *robot* long enough that they're starting to believe you weren't a real boy at all."

"What? The film?" Cage stepped off the bed. He lowered the gun, and the bird glided off onto the dresser.

The jay said, "Yeah. In fact, that's why I'm here. I want to tell you about the Animal Academy Awards, among other things."

Cage put the shotgun on the bed.

Dirty pulled out his flask and settled down for a chat with the kid.

* * *

On the evening of the Animal Academy Awards, Itsy convinced Stinkin' to do some cocaine with him in the top-level VIP bathroom of the Opera House.

After a dog-sized line, Stinkin' leaned out of the alcove that looked down upon the seated animals and yelled, "Wooooooooooooooooo! I'm a mutha fuckin' king-ass rat! Bow down, bitches! Bow down!"

Itsy pulled the rat back into the bathroom. "Chill out," he growled.

"Aw, fuck it, Itsy! We *rule*!" Stinkin' ran a few circles and chewed on his tail.

The dog shook his head while he peed. He muttered, "Should *not* have given the rat coke."

Stripey and Scaredy snickered from inside a stall.

"Is Dirty here, yet? He needs some of that coke." Stinkin' chewed his tail.

"He's not, and he does not. All I need is that dumbass bird all whacked out on this shit." Itsy finished peeing and checked himself in the mirror.

He pulled his boss over beside him, popped his tail out of his mouth and gave him some gum. "Chill out, boss.

It's your big night."

Stinkin' said, "It's *your* big night, Itsy. After this, you'll fuck every bitch in town, out of town and around town. You could even fuck a human!" The rat hopped up and down.

The cats laughed.

The rats laughed.

The chickens laughed through the vent between the female and male restrooms.

Itsy babysat his boss-rat during the Awards, even after doing a few more blasts of coke and six shots of tequila himself. He took care of the amped out, extra obnoxious, extra crude, extra assy rodent until the crew was called to the stage for the second time that night to receive an award— Best FX. After that, Itsy was dead.

But first he made half of a speech.

It went something like this:

"Thank you. Thank you. I want to thank my crew for their work on the FX. Without them, the movie's realistic boy would never have walked. Or cried, or begged for mercy. I mean, those rats and chickens... Those rats..." He looked to Stinkin', who was spacing out and trying to gain some composure.

Itsy lost focus for a moment—the audience blurring into fur and fog. He let dizziness roll and pass over him.

He continued, "I fucking hate people. I hate them! That boy. That boy's parents..."

The audience started murmuring. Camera flashes winked and blared. The crew looked around at each other. Stinkin' turned slowly to Itsy.

Itsy loomed over the microphone at the podium. He glared into the audience and spit when he began raving, "Are you all so stupid? Herd beasts! Pavlovian idiots! Robotics?! Are you serious? Do you really believe that?" His eyes bugged from his little Yorkie head. He screamed, "Cage is a real boy!"

The dog paused for the collective gasp of the crowd

before he went on. "That's not FX! I used to live with that little fucker!" Itsy foamed and ranted. "His dad beat me! Beat me every day. For no fucking reason! I ran away and lived on the street for five years. When I got a job across the street from that house, I thought it I'd take a shit on the porch, or piss on their vegetables. But then Cage came along and discovered us. We kidnapped him. *I* kidnapped him!"

The murmur of the audience grew rapidly to growling, cawing, hooting, snarling, yelling and demanding. Animals were on their feet. Security pigs stood on their hind hooves and waved their clubs. Cameras flashed faster than ever.

Isty kept talking while the crew tried to drag him away from the mic.

Stagehands from stage left rushed onstage.

Stinkin' screamed, "He's lying! It's a joke! A JOKE!"

Itsy panted into the microphone, "He's real! He's! He's—holy shit, he's right *there*!" The dog—suspended in the air, holding the podium with his claws and being dragged away by Scaredy and Stripey—suddenly tore in half as a gun blast echoed through the Opera House.

Itsy yelped into the microphone, gurgled, and died.

The cats fell to the floor holding onto the bottom half of the dog. They were covered in guts and blood.

The audience screamed.

Cage appeared from stage right, hefting a sawed-off shotgun and blasting at the film crew with hate and vengeance. His father strode beside him with two pistols blazing. Each human carried multiple weapons on their person, strapped, stuffed and stuck on. Cage had a backpack packed with Molotov cocktails.

Their eyes were steel and evil.

They emptied their anger onto the animals.

Stinkin' Rat was smeared across the stage with the second blast from Cage's shotgun. He didn't even have a chance to scream an obscenity. Scaredy dropped Itsy's bloody bottom half, and hissed. Cage blew his head off and most of Stripey's chest with the next shot.

His father was screaming. Sometimes words formed out of his punctuating shouts, but mostly they were guttural, anguished sounds that followed each report from his 9mms. When he ran out of ammo, he dropped the pistols and pulled his own shortened shotguns from his back.

Stinkin' Productions was dead. Bodies lay across the stage. Bloody feathers floated through the spot lit air. Only Stripey still twitched, and that was an automatic response to having most of his heart removed.

A security pig jumped on the stage in front of the boy. His father put two holes in the pig's head. Cage kicked the thrashing pig while he blasted the other two security pigs over the edge of the stage.

Cage did not say a word. He stepped methodically over dying or dead animals and shot chickens, rats, cats, squirrels, robins, voles, dogs and whatever else presented itself for shooting. The boy and his father killed the stagehands running off stage. They shot the stork camera operators, the animal press that were in the front row, the rooster MC, the squirrel dance team and the seagulls that had announced the award-winners.

Father and son walked off stage reloading and shooting animals that fled or hid. They'd already hacked up the hands, prompters and director. The humans slowly made their way toward the main exit as animals ran ahead of them. They opened doors and shot randomly into rooms. They lit fires.

Cage and his dad caught up with a large section of the audience crammed into the main foyer where the humans had entered, killed the pig guards with towel-wrapped pistols, locked the doors and built a barricade of furniture for just this occasion.

They opened fire from the top of the steps leading up to the foyer.

Cage tossed Molotov cocktails into the crowd while his dad let go with his semi-automatic rifles. Then he took out his pistols. The humans slaughtered the room of animals.

There were sounds no one has ever heard, and sounds no one ever will. There were sights that separated Cage from childhood forever. There were smells of death, barbeque and gunfire.

Cage and his father tore the remaining barricades down, unlocked the door and made their way out of the Opera House through the long twisting tunnel. They stepped into the black night behind Reeves Middle School, got into their truck and drove out of town.

The humans arrived at the former offices/studio/apartments of Stinkin' Productions, tripped the trigger for the secret garage and pulled in behind the animals' van.

The duo marched silently through the underground complex, straight to Stinkin's room.

Cage's dad pulled the rug from the floor, overturning the rat's bed and revealing a trapdoor.

Cage slid the door aside and he and his father descended a staircase into the bomb shelter sub basement where they ransacked Stinkin's treasure trove, taking all the original copies of *A Boy Named Cage* and its unedited footage. They took the footage for the zombie film, too—including the zombie-cat attack in the dining room.

Everything was just as Dirty Bird had said it would be.

The humans drove home in silence. They burned their gory clothes, took showers and went to sleep.

CHAPTER EIGHT
Dark Night of the Soul

Cage didn't speak for two weeks. He stayed in his room with the curtains drawn and the door closed. He spent most of his time painting forests, oceans and deserts empty of animals on the walls of his room.

The only time anyone heard his voice was when he acted out elaborate dreams while sleepwalking. The nocturnal plays mostly involved unspeakable animal acts, but sometimes they had nothing to do with the boy's recent experiences.

A few nights, Cage spoke as if he were possessed. In fact, he told his parents that he *was* possessed. He claimed to be alien travelers from hundreds of thousands of light years away, projecting their consciousness across the stars to interact with fellow intelligences. The aliens only visited three times.

Their final visit ended with Cage booming in a low, unnatural voice, "You people are a bunch of inane douchebags!"

But that wasn't the end of the dream-plays.

Cage dreamt about Courtney. He acted out dreams about driving, being a rockstar, going to school naked, catfish noodling, naked rockstar noodling, stand-up comedy (he was terrible and both of his parents heckled him), Yiffing with the Stars, climbing a spit-string onto the scabby lip of a Bangkok whore and being a mollusk.

While sleeping, Cage drove the car through the

garage door one night, slammed on the brakes, honked the horn and fell out into some rat traps on the lawn. He ate a bowl of teabags. He called North Korea and pissed them all off. He invested online and lost thousands.

His mother was panicked.

His father told her not to worry. The boy would come around. He just needed time.

"We *all* need time," he said, "and some new hobbies."

Cage's father started hunting every animal in the neighborhood. Cats, dogs, birds, hamsters, squirrels, raccoons, rats (especially rats), chickens and anything else he could find. He spent every night skulking through yards—poisoning, chopping, shooting, wringing, whatever it took.

His dad brought his prey home for food now and then. No one ate it but him.

Cage refused to eat meat.

His mother was frantic at that, having no idea what to feed the boy. She finally broke down and asked a dreadlocked person standing around in front of the Co-Op what vegetarians eat. She waited patiently for the dirty person to stop laughing and then followed his pointing finger inside. The girl in the deli was much more helpful.

But even lentils, tofu and eleventy-seven varieties of greens couldn't make her little boy into the glowing cherub he'd been.

Cage kept his curtains drawn. He stared at the murals on his walls. When he finally started talking, he didn't speak to any of his friends. He barely watched TV.

His father came to his room every night with guns, knives and snacks and asked Cage if he'd accompany him on a stroll through the neighborhood. Cage refused.

Cage's father stopped asking after a few weeks. It wasn't that he didn't want his son to reap a little of his own revenge. It was that the animals had started fighting back. Two pigs and a weasel attacked him as he came out the back door for one of his nightly forays. Had he not been holding his katana, he'd most likely have had his throat ripped out by that nasty weasel. As it was, the family had lots of ham.

Cage didn't eat it.

The boy lost weight. He developed circles under his eyes. He mumbled about assassins. He made a cave out of his blankets and stayed in it.

His dad tried to tell people what had happened.

Cage's father talked to a preacher, though he'd never been to his church. The preacher told him to pray. And to come to church. And that animals don't talk.

He talked to veterinarians and the weird lady down the street with twenty-six cats. When they only scoffed, he started telling anyone who'd listen to him for five minutes. The police questioned him about the abnormally large number of animal disappearances and mutilations happening in his neighborhood. He convinced them that two hundred dollars a week was much better than some stinky old animals.

Cage's father was at his wit's end. His wife was losing her shit day by day. She cooked ham all day long and drank Wild Turkey. His son was a fucking mushroom. Animals were after them. It was only a matter of time before they got into the house. He had to act.

Finally, without his son's permission or knowledge, Cage's dad contacted important people. Important people in the movie business. People who could tell him what to do with the most important film in the history of films.

One important person, an old friend that he'd run across on Facebook and who was an executive for a Big Time Movie Studio, agreed to view the movie.

Cage went with his dad to Hollywood after his father explained that the animals were mobilizing against their house, and that they had to go undercover and on the run or gain enough power that they were untouchable. He told Cage that they would let the truth be known to all of the world, that the animal conspiracy would be exposed and eradicated. He said being a movie star and hero of humanity was way better than hiding from every animal alive. Cage couldn't disagree.

The boy reluctantly agreed to meet with the Big Time Movie Studio people.

Cage's mom stayed behind to pack up the house. She worked on that for about two days. On the third day, she found herself sitting in the corner eating a box of stale cereal with kippered snacks mixed in. She was naked, the floor was covered in pee, and there was a notebook at her side with the word, *UKIRAH*, scrawled on it.

A squirrel at the window scratched threateningly at the glass. Cage's mother remembered something about mice flowing out of the bathtub faucet, skittering across the floor, crawling up her legs, nipping at her and chanting something that ended in, *Chop! Chop! Chop!* She remembered stomping and running. She remembered the phone being dead. She remembered screaming—taking pills and screaming.

She called some movers and went online to find the best mental institution in Hollywood. She took some more pills. She went to the spa toting a shotgun and daring any fucking animal to *come the fuck on and get some* as she made her way from house to car and car to spa.

* * *

Cage and his father were oblivious to his mother's tribulations. They were having adventures of their own.

When they arrived in the offices of the Big Time Movie Studio, the movie executive kept them waiting until he was forty-five minutes late for their meeting. He told them that because he was so late, they didn't really have time for much of a meeting, but that he'd view the opening of the film and listen to as much of the synopsis as possible. He said there was an important person due to arrive soon, and so could they please just show the movie.

Cage's dad, all flustered and pissed-off, but smart enough to not punch the important person in his important nose, started the movie.

A few minutes into the film, the executive paged his secretary and told her to clear his afternoon. Then he made some phone calls to some even *more* important people who came and viewed the film. The Big Time Movie Studio executive executives realized it was something that the world had never seen. For them that meant more power and money.

The execs wondered how the father and son team made the animals act so perfectly and what sort of animation had been used to make their mouths move so realistically when they spoke. They wanted to know the budget, and couldn't believe that a father and son team with virtually no money had produced the film.

So Cage's dad told them the true story.

They did not believe the true story until Cage had a breakdown in the movie executive's big conference room with lots of important people—screaming about how every animal was out to get him, and how he and his father had massacred all those innocent animals and that the birds were watching him—and Cage's father showed them the unedited footage of the actual abduction and subsequent plotting of the animals.

Even still, the movie executives didn't believe most of the story, but realized that something had happened during the film's creation to make Cage afraid of animals to a terrifying degree, and if they were going to get the kid to act in a sequel, they were going to have to do something about his zoophobia.

One older, wizened exec said, "Come on, zombie-cats?"

Deals were struck. Contracts were signed. Smiles were smiled. Cage's dad got on the phone and bought a big house.

It was decided that Cage would be sent to an uninhabited island in the Pacific to meet with a master of child-psychiatry, animal husbandry and making boys into men. They even paid to have all the crabs burned off the beach and enclosed the island with the largest net ever stitched.

The boy would stay until cured of his fear. Then he'd return to Hollywood to film the sequel.

* * *

A Boy Named Cage took the human world by storm. Box office records were broken. Action figures appeared in fast food meals for kids. Everyone wanted to be kidnapped by animals and turned into a pig. The soundtrack went platinum. Little girls swooned. PETA protested.

Cage became a movie star.

But he didn't know about his immense, intense, extreme, obscene, worldwide fame for five months. He spent the time of the movie's release and subsequent fame on an island with Arrrgh, the Wizard of Wisdom—as the animal-loving, man-making shrink liked to call himself. Among other things.

Cage knew nothing of the world outside the island during that time. Not even that his father had been run down and killed by a carload of chickens. It happened one Monday morning a week after the movie was released to the human public, when Cage's dad crossed the street from the sporting goods store to the bar.

CHAPTER NINE
On the Island, Off the Island

On the island, Cage was embraced, examined and emboldened by the mysterious Arrrgh—a man who hates microbes, microbrews and microwaves but not micro-bikinis. Cage learned how to smoke. He learned how to swear even better than before. He learned how to tell what a man's been eating by the smell of the sweat from his ass crack. He never learned why that is important.

Cage was flown to the island by helicopter and dropped through the cargo chute—a net-tube that led from a hole at the top of the island's giant surrounding net to the beach near Arrrgh's villa. Only one bird ever found its way into the cargo chute, and it was subsequently crushed by a delivery of pornographic magazines, seventy pounds of tanning lotion, a Real Doll and six-dozen jumbo cans of pork and beans.

The boy tumbled through the ninety-foot cargo chute. Arrrgh waited for him on the beach.

"Get up," said the psychiatrist/husbandrist/islander. He held out his manly manicured hand. "My name is Arrrgh—Sexiest Man Alive."

Cage let the man help him up. He looked around at the beach, villa and cliffside jungle.

"Eat this," said Arrrgh. He handed the boy a mushy green blob the size of a ping-pong ball.

Cage took the squishy thing. "What is it?"

"It's an ayahuasca-soaked peyote button. Eat it."

Cage ate it.

"So I hear you're afraid of animals," Arrrgh mentioned, guiding the boy to his villa.

Cage nodded at the wild-eyed, chest-haired, silver-thonged middle-aged man. He looked past Arrrgh to the beach. He saw snakes of water surfing across the waves.

"They said there aren't animals here," Cage whispered. He watched giant snakes threading themselves through the breaking ocean.

"There aren't."

"What about those snakes?" Cage pointed at the ocean. The sky lost its blue, and Cage could see its skin, way up there at the edge of the stars. It was heavy and smelled like lemons. His footsteps on the sand echoed. The snakes began to laugh.

Cage puked on his feet.

Arrrgh smiled and took the boy by the shoulder. "Oh, there are snakes in everything. You'll see. Want some pork and beans?"

Arrrgh hosed the boy off outside the villa, and they made their way to the kitchen.

Cage tried to eat pork and beans, but he thought about the pork, and the beans kept slipping out from between his lips. He mostly spit pork and beans.

Arrrgh watched him spit his food for a while and then said, "All right. Here, swallow this," he produced a small red nut and handed it to the boy.

"What is it?" Cage asked.

"It's an LSD/psilocybin/salvia-injected coffee bean. Swallow it."

Cage swallowed it.

Arrrgh stood. "Now just sit here until I come get you." He disappeared through a door.

Cage sat and tried to think. Beans began yelling up to him, and he shushed them, knowing there was something really important he was about to remember or discover. The bowl of beans began shrieking about snakes, and Cage looked down to see a writhing bowl of tiny snakes.

"Holy shit!" he yelled.

Arrrgh reappeared. He grabbed Cage by his t-shirt and dragged him out of the kitchen. "It's time for the puppet show!" he exclaimed.

The psychiatrist/puppeteer/pork and bean aficionado deposited Cage into the too-soft cushions of a floral-print loveseat.

Arrrgh stood in front of a puppet stage. "Now, Cage," he said, "I'm going to do a little puppet show for you. There are animal puppets in this show. I want you to remember that they are only puppets. They're puppets, Cage. Puppets. Cage. These animals are puppets. That's why they can talk. Okay, Cage? Puppets."

"Okay! Fucking puppets!"

Arrrgh stared at Cage for two minutes. "Oh. Yes. Not real animals. There are no animals on this island. Only fish."

"Fish don't talk?"

"Animals don't talk." Arrrgh ducked under the curtain.

Soon two puppets appeared onstage—a blue whale and a flying squirrel.

Arrrgh mumbled, "Oh," and the squirrel disappeared. Cage heard the sound of the play button on a cassette player being depressed, though being a thirteen-year-old in modern times he did not recognize it as such.

The flying squirrel shot back into view as tinny ska music began playing from under the puppet stage.

Cage started to *really* hallucinate.

Arrrgh wiggled his whaley hand and said in a deep stupid voice, "Oh, I'm a big whale. I'm bigger than anything. I could totally eat you. But I'm not going to because I'm nice. All animals are nice."

But the whale puppet *was* going to eat Cage.

It grew bigger and bigger with each dopey word that came from its out-of-synch mouth. Soon it ate the puppet stage, a lamp and a beanbag and loomed above Cage.

The boy screamed and tried to jump over the back of the couch.

"Wait," said the big dumb whale voice, "I'm nice. All animals are nice."

The whale swallowed Cage.

Its mouth was black and felty. It was a rough ride down to the belly of the big puppet whale. Cage sensed someone sliding down beside him. He found a hand and held onto it. He screamed beside who he could only assume was Arrrgh.

Finally Cage and his companion tumbled into the whale's stomach.

"What happened?" asked Cage.

"Hold on."

Cage heard Arrrgh rustling around with something. Soon a flashlight shone around the vast felt belly.

"Wow," said the boy. He followed the beam from the light. It faded into darkness, never touching upon a surface.

There was no sloshing stomach acid in the whale's belly. There was felt. Black felt. Cage sat on it.

Arrrgh played the light around. Only the wall where they were dumped out and the parts where they stood were visible.

The boy asked, "So do we just walk out? I mean, there's probably just a big hole at the end of the whale puppet. We're not moving."

"Oh, we're moving. We're *always* moving."

"I think we should walk."

Arrrgh handed the flashlight to Cage. "Hold this."

Cage took the flashlight and shone it toward where he thought the end of the puppet must be. He heard Arrrgh rummaging around again.

When he shone the light on Arrrgh, Cage found he was holding up two puppets.

"Still have Cody, the flying squirrel. And this is his buddy—Tripp." He wiggled a bulldog puppet. "Ruff!"

"What?" Cage shone the light on the man's face.

Arrrgh squinted and ducked. He shook the bulldog puppet. "Rere, rake rhis," he said.

Cage said, "Dogs don't really talk like that." He took what the puppet-dog held in its mouth.

Cody pushed a lighter at Cage.

The boy held up a cigarette. "What's this?"

Arrrgh said, "It's marijuana, valerian, catnip, ergot, hemlock, blue orchid, black poppy and tobacco. Smoke it."

"I've never smoked." Cage looked at the cigarette. He dropped the lighter.

"Oh, give me that!" Arrrgh snatched the flashlight from the boy and searched for the lighter. When he found it, he shook the puppets off his hands, nestled the flashlight between his shoulder and cheek, took the joint from the kid and lit it.

The shrink took a hit and handed the doobie to Cage. "Just suck it in and hold it." He bent and retrieved the puppets.

Cage took the joint, sucked and coughed out a huge cloud. The beam of the flashlight was suddenly white with smoke.

Arrrgh exhaled. "Hit it again."

The boy toked.

After a few hits, he coughed less. He said, "What about the ash?"

Arrrgh held out an ashtray.

Cage ashed and took another hit. The blackness in the whale's stomach began to lighten toward gray. Arrrgh put the ashtray down beside Cage.

Suddenly the boy asked, "Hey, where do you keep

getting all this stuff?"

The man replied, "I, uh, brought it with me."

"In your pockets?"

"Yes."

"But you're only wearing a bikini bottom."

"Yes. Take another hit."

He did.

Arrrgh sat beside the boy, resting his puppeted hands on his knees. "Cage, animals can't really talk. Only puppet animals can. I'm going to help you to see that. I'm going to show you that whatever you thought you experienced was a form of hysteria. It was most likely brought about by your true abductors whom I'm sure did all sorts of sexually deviant things with you and animals, which of course we'll speak about in great detail. For now, I want you to concentrate on the fact that all animals are good, except microbes but they hardly count as animals being so nasty and small and creepy and ugly and stupid. All animals are good. We'll talk about that more. You'll be here with me for a while. We'll have plenty of time to talk about animals being good and nice and not talking. Smoke that."

Cage heard whale song through cotton and Arrrgh's words above the muted music like the shamanistic truths of a dried up hermit in a desert cave. He began to believe.

The bulldog and flying squirrel started to dance.

The whale's belly grew brighter and brighter.

Cage took a hit and looked toward the end of the whale puppet. A light shone there. It became larger.

Cage said, "The whale is going to poop us out."

The flying squirrel puppet said, "Hell yes, it is. That's what whales do when they accidentally eat you. Because whales are nice. All animals are nice."

Tripp joined his friend, "Rup. Re'll roop rus right rout."

"What?"

70

"I said, all animals are nice."

The whale puppet pooped them out. They were dumped back into Arrrgh's living room. The whale puppet lay on an ottoman.

"Sorry," it said in its dumb whale voice.

"It's okay," said Cage, "you're just a puppet."

Electric snakes curled in the air beside Arrrgh. He said, "And now I make you a man."

After a feast of fish tacos, pork and beans, fish pizza, barbeque chips, fish loaf, pita, goat cheese, fish lasagna and shots of tequila, Arrrgh got straight to work making Cage into a man.

He handed him a tall drink.

"What's this?" Cage asked.

"Vodka, ether, absinthe, birch-bark beer, diesel, corn syrup, LSD and coffee. Drink it."

Cage drank it.

Months passed.

Cage didn't know that months were passing. The mancoction that Arrrgh fed the boy tipped him over the edge of reality. Time bent comfortably to his perception.

The psychiatrist/mixologist/misogynist kept the boy in a dreamy, timeless state. Arrrgh fed Cage coconut jelly and nettle butter. He kept him hydrated. He molded his little boy mind into something more suitable for a man.

Through Arrrgh's patented reprogramming process, Cage not only became a man, but he became a man afraid of no animal. This, in the end, is ridiculous.

There are animals out there that you should be afraid of, even if they've got nothing so personally against you such as you having murdered a couple hundred of their fellow film-loving animals—not to mention movie stars, news crews, artists, writers, and the greatest production team in all of animal history, even if that production team was a bunch of outlaws who kidnapped you and tortured you and made a movie about it which is what made them so fucking great in the first place.

So even if every animal in the world *doesn't* hate you and want you dead, you should be afraid of animals like bad-ass monster sharks, alligators with swords, rabid snakes, crack-bears and poisonous *anythings*.

Arrrgh made an animal-loving man out of Cage. With all the hallucinogenic drugs the shrink pumped into the kid while he hypnotized him to believe that all animals are cute little things that need to be pet or cuddled or kissed, Arrrgh was quite successful in helping the boy to forget the truth of what had happened to him.

Cage soon found it a crazy idea that animals could talk. He laughed out loud—as opposed to laughing in silence—when Arrrgh talked about Aslan, Wilbur, Mr. Ed or Scooby.

Eventually the man-maker/animal-lover/germaphobe allowed Cage to come down off his big weird drug trip. Arrrgh let his programming take hold while Cage spent a week in a beach bungalow with the shrink's newest Real Doll and a few cans of pork and beans.

After a ceremony under the New Moon involving two-man slam-dancing to their own beat-boxing, cutting the net surrounding the island and singing *inviting songs* for dolphins, crabs, octopi and iguanas but not for urchins or sharks because they'd come anyway, Arrrgh declared Cage cured. He gave him a certificate of manhood, a slap on the ass and saw him off the next morning as the boy sailed away on the Studio's yacht.

Nearly half a year after tumbling through the cargo chute onto the beach and eating that weird green thing that the King of Men and Beasts fed him, a more manly, less frightened thirteen-year-old Cage returned to Hollywood. He was tan, stupid and happy—in perfect condition for stardom. He landed a book deal, a shoe deal and a deal on his minor infractions of drunk driving (without a license) and soliciting a prostitute.

Cage bought a big house, new clothes, and some friends. He paid for his mother to have extra medication and an extra luxurious room in her mental institution. He went to his father's grave and gave him a twenty-one gun salute—by himself.

The boy-star flew back to L.A. in his new private jet and immersed himself in *the scene*. Paris Hilton got all cougar on him, and he spent a week clubbing with her and her dogs—who dropped acid in his drink as often as they could and peed in his shoes. They didn't kill him, though they thought about it. They kept an eye on him for the animal police.

In general, the animals wanted him dead, but they wanted him to answer for his crimes in court. They wanted everything legal. They couldn't draw attention to themselves, and the boy was surrounded by security. The animal police waited, even while vigilante groups formed.

After a brief tour of talk shows and a Spring Break fling with MTV, the Big Time Movie Studio execs wrangled Cage into the filming of the sequel to their industry-bending, hugely successful hit. They began pre-production of *A Pig Named Cage.*

CHAPTER TEN
The Sequel

The Big Time Movie Studio held a meet-and-greet get-together for the cast and crew of *A Pig Named Cage*. They held it on-set so everyone could get a feel for the upcoming shoot as well as acquaint themselves with the numerous animals with which they'd be working.

The animal trainers and handlers put on a show with the animal actors after everyone loosened up with drinks and highlights from *A Boy Named Cage* and some of the music videos from its soundtrack, broadcast on flat-screen TVs hung throughout the set.

Cage would work with nearly every animal in the film, so the handlers chose him to interact with the animals during the introductory show.

He rode piggy-back on a bear.

He lay down and was covered by an army of ants who swept across his body in perfect marching formations from head to feet and side to side.

Cage was introduced to a nervous skunk, a purple crab, a meth-addicted scorpion, a narcoleptic egret and a troupe of acrobatic bats—all of whom had some cute thing to do with Cage. The boy loved it, having come to adore everything about every animal. Most of the animals loathed it, each of them wishing to do something nasty to the boy and none of them being able to.

It was the opening party where the animal actors got together and talked about the murderous human.

After all the humans had gone home, passed-out or were involved in the orgy that was going on in the leading-lady's triple-wide trailer, the animals got together and had their own pre-production meeting.

Happy, the perpetually pissed-off brown bear, said, "Accidents happen all the time. Shit, bears kill people in the woods—that's what we do. I can accidentally kill him."

"No you can't," said Mark, the egret. "They'll kill you right back. And he's gotta answer for his crimes publicly."

Adolf, one of the sixty-eight thousand, four hundred and twelve ants named Adolf, piped up through his little ant megaphone, "*We* can kill him. They'll never get all of us!"

"How are you going to kill him?" asked Blind-Ass Bat. "You're not even poisonous."

Adolf's antennae straightened. He yelled into his megaphone, "We'd crawl down his miserable human throat and choke him to death. Or eat his brains through his ear."

"We're not going to kill him!" yelled Mark.

"Nope," said The Fumigator. She hopped her skunk-butt up on a director's chair. "We're not going to kill him. We're going to steal him."

"What?" Happy asked.

"What?" asked eleven bats and sixty-eight thousand, four hundred and twelve ants in unison.

Whats abounded.

The Fumigator settled everyone down by clearing her throat. "Happy, you still have those connections in Yellowstone?"

"The ground squirrels? Sure."

"And they can get us into Canada?" The Fumigator asked.

"They can," the bear answered.

The other animals began chattering.

The skunk cleared her throat again and addressed the animals. "I think we should kidnap Cage and take him to

Toronto. We can make our own movie. It's what we've been talking about."

From out of the swirling animal talk came the bear's voice, "Fumy, this isn't what we've been talking about. We've been talking about making our own movie about making movies."

The skunk smiled wide and spread her paws. "Don't you see? This is the ultimate expression of that. Stinkin' Productions' film was ground-breaking, even before we knew the boy was real. A huge success. After the kid stole the movie, the humans called it their own and pretended that the animals in it were actors. The film is a huge sensation in the human world, too. And it was filmed by animals!

"We're the animals hired to star in the human sequel. If we steal the kid during its filming, and make our own film about that abduction, we'll be one-upping everyone. We'll be making our own sequel. We'll ride the wave and be the next giants to rise from the mayhem of this whole strange situation. We'll be legends!" The Fumigator jumped up and down in the chair.

The bats said, "She's right!"

The ants cheered.

Happy nodded thoughtfully, his paw on his chin.

Mark frowned, but didn't say anything negative.

Steven the scorpion snapped out of his reverie. "Fuck yeah, let's *kill* that human! I'm in! I'll sting that fucker's eyeballs!" He went skittering around in circles, flicking his stinger.

"Calm down, Steven," said Mark, "we've got a new plan." He fell asleep.

The Crab Formerly Known as King asked, "Isn't it illegal to kidnap a human?"

The skunk smiled. "Not this one. It's only illegal to let humans know that we can speak and operate machinery and all that. Cage *knows* already. We're not breaking any laws. Not any animal laws."

"But he's wanted by the police," said Burk Bat.

"Fuck those slugs!" yelled Steven. He flicked his stinger.

The Fumigator said, "Calm down, Steven. We'll turn him over to the police when we're done with him."

"Why Canada?" shouted an Adolf.

Happy answered, "Because it's cheaper to film there and Toronto looks pretty much like any city in the U.S."

"That's right," said The Fumigator, "and no one's gonna look for the kid there."

"How would we get to Yellowstone with all our equipment?" asked Barton Bat.

"Yeah, that's pretty far," worried Crab.

"We'll drive," answered awakened Mark.

"Drive?" The bats asked together.

Happy raised a big bear paw. "I can drive," he told the animals. "I'll get us there."

The Fumigator bounced up and down smiling. "So, do we do it?"

Animal actors looked to one another. There were hushed and heated discussions. It was their dream. Opportunity had arisen. Yellowstone is a great place to visit in early September. They decided to do it.

Plans were planned.

* * *

The third day of shooting involved a scene where Cage was wrestling Happy. The boy would best the beast, tame him, and ride him around the forest, gathering an animal army to defeat the Legion of Giant Squid—Interlopers from the Sea.

The Big Time Movie Studio didn't actually have any living giant squid, so they'd shot some footage off the coast of

Baja, Mexico the month before. Baja Squid are exceptionally nasty and hate humans more than most animals, even in the lawless sea. Two cameramen lost hands during the filming of the squid scenes, which provided excellent footage of squid attacks, but was hell on the insurance.

Being a closed set, there were relatively few humans inside. It proved simple for the animals to drug the food, water, and toilet paper. After the lunch break, during the third take of the scene, all of the humans began passing out.

Those that had not wiped, eaten, or drank water on-set were fairly easily incapacitated—being two wardrobe girls and an aged actor. Having a big brown bear on their team stacked the odds in the animals' favor. They tied the humans together, took their phones and left them in a trailer, much to the old actor's unexpected pleasure.

The animals put Cage on a couch from the actor's lounge and slid him to the center of their staging area.

The Fumigator, Happy, two bats and The Crab Formerly Known as King headed to makeup. Two bats and Mark manned cameras and filmed the crew at work while the other animals guarded doors, gathered equipment and loaded it into golf carts. The ants hefted their mobile colony—a large Tupperware bin filled with dirt and sticks—and carried it across the bay.

When The Fumigator and crew came out of makeup, the other animals were shocked to see what a great job they'd done making Happy into a human. A sloppy, fat human—but a human nonetheless.

Happy couldn't speak, because that would pull his head out of his shirt and move the mask in front of his eyes. His head was a little longer than most people's, but not grotesquely so. His paws featured human-hand gloves. He was dressed in a blue button-down shirt and blue slacks. He wore a nametag that said, *Bus Driver Bob*.

He wobbled on his hind legs to the wide bay doors.

Bryana Bat pushed the button that opened them.

"Break a leg!" shouted The Fumigator as Happy walked off the set and onto the lot.

The sun shone in a terrible rectangle on the floor.

Bryana closed the doors behind the bear.

The animals waited.

They lined up the golf carts near the bay doors and made certain Cage was still alive. They triple-checked their equipment lists. They destroyed vending machines for snacks. A couple bats did it in the rafters.

Soon came the signal—two blasts of a big-ass horn.

Bryana opened the doors.

Happy backed-in a tourist bus.

The bat closed the door behind him, and the animals got to work loading their new vehicle with film-making equipment and their sleeping prisoner.

After twenty minutes, Happy snarled through clenched teeth, "Hurry, I gotta get outta this mask!"

Forty-three minutes after Happy the angry bear toddled out into the sunlight, crept into an empty, idling tour bus and pulled it into their pirated set, the animals set out in their ark with Bus Driver Bob at the wheel.

Once on the freeway, Happy tore off the mask. "Phew!" he exclaimed. "Get. Me. A beer!"

CHAPTER ELEVEN
The Big Chase Scene

Cage was on Paris' vibrating bed again. It reminded him of all the other times he'd come awake there, sharing the pink comforter with her cute little dogs. He wondered why she always left it vibrating—it was pretty jarring, really. Probably to waste electricity.

He reached for Paris, snaking an arm between her spindly legs. She squawked and flapped her wings at him.

Cage opened his eyes.

A big white bird slapped at him. "Let go of my junk!" it screamed.

The bird jumped across the aisle between seats on a bus. It landed on a snoozing skunk who screamed something in French. Cage looked from the skunk to the seat in front of it where a purple crab poked its eye-stalks and claws around the seatback. Bats fluttered around the roof of the bus, shouting about letting them sleep. Trees sped past through the windows.

"You can talk!" yelled the boy. And Cage's life came rushing back upon him.

He fell to the floor of the bus and curled into a ball while the entire ordeal of the previous year and a half played through his mind. He began sobbing uncontrollably.

"Shut that kid up!" yelled the bus driving bear.

Mark recovered enough to start filming.

The Fumigator hopped down beside the boy and tried to calm him with a song about scent glands and secretions, but he only cried harder.

Burgermeister Bat landed on Cage's shoulder. He

said, "Come on kid. It'll be okay."

The boy stopped sobbing. He choked out, "That's what all animals say."

"Yeah, fuck it," said Steven, pacing the back of a seat. "Let's kill the fucker."

Cage cowered and screamed.

"We're not going to kill you," said The Fumigator.

"We will if you don't shut up!" yelled Happy.

That's when the sirens started blaring behind the bus.

"Shit!" shouted the bear, stomping on the gas pedal.

Steven skidded down the aisle yelling, "Fuck man! Do the drugs! Do the drugs!" He ran to his little scorpion backpack and started ripping open baggies with his pincers.

"How many?" asked The Fumigator, moving beside the bear.

"A lot," he answered, growling and pushing the bus to go faster. Cars ahead of him skidded out of the way, most of them just in time. He bumped the back of a minivan and it shot off into the median, skidding to a stop in a swirl of dust. A cop car halted beside it.

A police cruiser drove up in the other lane fast. The heavily tinted windows kept the identity of the passengers obscured, but the driver's window was untinted.

Happy yelled, "Fumy, get the mask!"

She handed it over, helping him adjust the neck and jumping down just as the cops pulled alongside.

The cops motioned for Bus Driver Bob to pull the bus over. Bob slowly shook his head no. He smashed into the back of a Mazda Miata. It stuck to the front of the bus, slowing it enough that the cop car shot ahead.

Happy swerved toward the cruiser, and the Miata shook loose. The tiny car spun into the opposing lane and clipped the back of the cop car. The cruiser spun out of control, off the highway and into a field, where it flipped onto its side and skidded to a halt against a big pine tree. The tumbling Miata slammed into the two lead chase vehicles following the bus. All three cars flipped into the air and broke to bits. Fires leapt to life.

Two cop cars still pursued, but they had to maneuver through the wreckage before trying to catch up to the bus.

"Holy fuckin' shit!" screamed Happy.

"Woooooo!" shouted the bats, flipping around the speeding bus.

"Helicopter?" asked the bear.

The animals searched out the windows. They could see no choppers.

"Only in the movies!" shouted Batshit-Crazy Bat, cartwheeling above the seats.

"Not true!" shouted Bean-Chucking Bat, catching Batshit-Crazy and tossing her toward the back of the bus.

"Shut up, bats!" growled the bear. To The Fumigator, he said quietly, "I'm starting to doubt the wisdom of this plan."

The skunk winked at the bear and looked toward the back of the bus. The approaching sirens grew louder. She yelled, "We're filming, right?"

Mark yelled back, "Rolling!"

Boston Cream Bat hollered back, "My camera's on!"

"Oh, crap, what's this?" yelled Bus Driver Bear.

A semi truck slowed down in front of them and began swerving across both lanes of the highway.

"Ram it!" yelled Burk Bat.

"Ram it?!" Happy screamed.

"Ram it!" affirmed the skunk.

He rammed it.

As the truck swerved to the left, Happy accelerated into it. The bus tore through the trailer snapping it from its hitch and tottering the cab onto its side. Cargo exploded as the truck broke apart under the charging bus. Illegal immigrants flew into the air, falling to the ground in a screaming rain.

People thudded onto the highway. They smacked into

the back of the bus and fell onto the cop cars. The cops ran a lot of them over, trying to stop before they came to the wreckage of the eighteen-wheeler. Not even a dozen bodies stopped the cops from smashing into the twisted truck, and both of their cars flipped end-over-ends to crunch and skid across the asphalt. The truck exploded—killing its surviving cargo, the driver, and the two living cops in the upturned cruisers.

The bus, suffering one flat tire, sped on.

"Where are we, anyway?" The Fumigator pulled the mask from Happy's head.

"Idaho."

"Idaho?" asked the skunk. "That was a quick trip."

"You were all asleep," Happy answered.

"Where are you taking me?" yelled Cage from the back of the bus.

"We're going to see Old Faithful, or some such natural wonder," answered Bean-Chucking Bat.

"Yellowstone?" asked the boy.

The Fumigator slid down the aisle. "Yes, Yellowstone," she said. "And from there to Canada." The skunk turned back to the bear. "How far to Yellowstone?" she asked him.

"Thirty-five miles."

"Canada?" Cage asked.

"Yes," said The Fumigator, "to make a movie."

"A movie?" Cage looked to the egret and bats with cameras. "Oh, no."

"We can make it!" shouted all the ants at once.

Another tire blew out. The bus wavered but kept going.

"Where have you Adolfs been?" asked Mark, swinging his camera toward the army marching down the aisle.

An Adolf with a megaphone shouted, "*Someone* packed our colony in the luggage compartment under the bus after our *one* pit-stop in Nevada. The vibration—and lack of food—lulled us to sleep. It wasn't until all the explosions that we woke up. Then we had to make our way up here, and

83

organize... Is there anything to eat?"

Mark fell asleep. The camera dangled in his wing.

Steven fell from the ceiling. The ants caught him and tossed him up onto a seat. He lay there unmoving.

"Steven's dead," said Brellina Bat.

"Why aren't there cops on our ass?" Happy yelled.

"Roadblock?" ventured The Crab Formerly Known as King.

"Roadblock," Happy said.

"Roadblock," The Fumigator mused.

"No! Roadblock!" shouted the bear. He pressed his foot to the gas. "Put the mask on me, Fumy! I'm goin' through!"

Ahead of them, on a curve in the road just before a bridge crossing a wide, shallow river, two Idaho State Police cars were parked nose-to-nose blocking the highway. Troopers stood behind the cars, and two more troopers stood behind two more cruisers parked on either side of the road.

The skunk shoved the mask on the bear, yelling, "Get a camera up here and film this action!"

"Everybody get down!" Happy shouted, shifting gears. The bus accelerated.

Mark awoke and they filled him in by screaming to shut up and get down. Then from The Fumigator, "Get up here and film this!"

Most everyone but Mark got on the floor or ducked behind seats. The bats running the camera perched on a seat back, balancing with their flapping wings. Mark duck-walked down the aisle and held his camera up with his wingtips, hoping that it was pointed straight at the action. He slid behind the driver's seat.

Bullets began clinking into the bus. A star of broken glass appeared on the windshield.

"Happy?" screamed The Fumigator.

"I'm good!" yelled the bear through clenched jaws as more bullets spattered into the bus.

The troopers unloaded as many rounds as they could as the bus bore down on them, but neither they nor their cars were a match for the speeding monster and its maniacal bear driver. The cops behind the blockade dove out of the way just as the bus tore into the cars, ripping each cruiser nearly in half.

The troopers on the sides of the highway shot at the retreating bus before jumping into their cars and attempting to maneuver past the burning wreckage of the roadblock cruisers. The location of the roadblock and the position of the wreckage made crossing the bridge on the highway impossible.

The burning cruisers exploded as the bus chugged slowly up the highway just past the river, headed over a mountain pass. The animals watched the cops hop around trying to figure out a way around their flaming roadblock as the bus whined its bullet-ridden way up the mountain.

The ants cheered.

The bats took to the air.

"Is everyone okay?" asked The Fumigator. "Anyone shot?"

The bus made it to the top of the mountain, and Happy eased back in his seat as they started down the other side. "I am," he answered. "Just a little." He pointed to his neck.

The skunk climbed his seat and gently peeled off the Bob mask. She found the wound. Gingerly, she pulled the bear's coarse hair out of the way. He shifted gears and grunted.

"Happy?" asked the skunk.

"Yes?"

"How far to Yellowstone?" She ruffed the fur around the wound.

He grunted and looked at the odometer. "About thirty—yeeeeoowch!"

The Fumigator pulled the chunk of windshield from the bear's neck. "No bullet," she told him, holding up the glass.

Happy smiled. "We're almost there," he said.

Fifteen minutes later, Happy swung the bus off the highway at an old rest area. He drove behind the decrepit toilets and onto a crumbling old road that slid off into the trees—the secret back entrance to Yellowstone.

CHAPTER TWELVE
Geysers are Really Fucking Hot

"Are we really going to Old Faithful?" Mark asked Happy.

The bear turned to the camera. "No, you dumbass."

"But we're going to a geyser."

The bear sighed and rolled his eyes. He cranked the steering wheel to round a sharp corner. "Yes, we're going to a geyser."

"Cool," said Mark. "What's it called?"

Happy growled, "For Gaia's sake! It's called Devil Whale's Blow Hole. It's a secret geyser that mostly only animals know about. The bison and eagles guard it from humans as best they can. Now get that camera out of my face! I'm trying to drive!"

Mark turned off the camera and strode to the back of the bus.

Cage watched the tall white bird walk past. The boy was having flashbacks from his time with the first film crew. He sat in his seat and watched the back of the bear's furry brown head. He cried silently, remembering Filthy Pig and Itsy and the toilet room.

Like most everyone else, Cage soon drifted into a sleeping sort of daze as trees whipped past dark windows and the flapping of shredded tires against the wheel-wells beat a throbbing rhythm through the sides of the bullet-puckered bus.

Just as Cage was falling asleep, a voice whispered in his ear suggesting that he visit the toilet. He stood and surveyed the surrounding seats. All the animals were sleeping or staring out the windows. Even the bats hung from the rails of the luggage racks, bobbing with the bus in their sleep. He couldn't tell who'd spoken to him.

Cage went to the toilet. When he did, he found a note taped to the mirror. It pointed him to a package under the sink.

Half an hour later, Happy called over his shoulder, "We're almost there! I'm going to pull over and we'll walk the rest of the way."

Once the animals were unloaded with minimal filming equipment, Happy led them through the trees on a barely visible trail toward a gently sloping ridge.

As they started off, The Fumigator said to the boy, "Don't try and escape. You're surrounded by animals. *Wild* animals. And they hate you more than we do."

Cage glared down at the skunk. He thought about kicking her, but stayed his kicking foot with all his will. Instead he said, "Whatever you say, stinky. If you hate me so much, why go through all this trouble to save me?"

"Because you're our meal ticket, kid. You're our way into the big Big Time."

"But there are a thousand boys like me."

"Millions," said the skunk, "but only one you."

"Here we are," announced the bear.

The animals and boy walked into a clearing in the forest. A mound of colorful mud rose twenty feet from the forest floor in step-like bubbled formations. Steaming water poured down the sides of the geyser-built mud tower.

"We meet your friends here?" The Crab Formerly Known as King sidled over to the stream of geyser water surrounding the formation like a moat. He dipped a claw and the tip turned bright red. "Yeowch!" he screamed.

"We meet my friends here," Happy answered, shaking his big bear head.

Just then, a ground squirrel appeared on the first step of the formation. He yelled, "Send the boy up here. We want to be sure he's real. And that he is who you say he is."

"Noah? Is that you?" Happy took a step toward the geyser.

"It's me," said the ground squirrel. "Now send up the kid."

Happy turned and snatched the boy by his arms. He swung Cage toward the mud tower. "Go up there," he said.

The bats flew a circle above the boy, and then shot off in the opposite direction, chasing after a swarm of grasshoppers. The ants stood in formation behind the crab and the skunk.

Cage went up the side of the mud tower, slipping and crying out about it being hot.

"Follow me," said the ground squirrel when Cage reached the top.

The boy turned and looked back at the gathered animals.

"Go on!" yelled the bear.

Cage walked over the mound and out of sight.

Happy said to The Fumigator, "He'll be right back. Those guys are above-board, fair, square and their word is good. They just want to be sure he is who we say he is."

"Why do they care?" asked the skunk.

"What?"

"Why do they care who he is? Aren't they just supposed to get us and our equipment across the border and set us up on the other side? Didn't we pay them to not ask questions? Why do they even have to know about—"

A rumbling, rushing sound cut her off.

The crab skittered up the bear's leg, "What's that?!" he yelled.

Water shot from behind the mud tower. A great gush of boiling water. It blasted thirty feet into the air—a fountain as thick as six bears the size of Happy. The animals scattered as magma-hot water poured down on them.

Even over their squeals, roars, chitters and swearing of surprise, every animal could hear the shrieking of a human boy.

The boiled bodies of ground squirrels thumped down around the actors. The steaming water stopped shooting from the mound before them, but continued to burn as it rained down. The animals heard a horrible keening from the other side of the mud tower.

The bats came flying back and landed in the trees facing the geyser.

The Crab Formerly Known as King was dead. His claws held him fast to the back of Happy's hind leg, but he was gone—boiled red. Happy shucked him off.

The ants were boiled, drowned little dams in the rivulets of geyser water that ran toward lower ground, or buried.

Cage came clamoring over the mound of mud.

The burning rain subsided.

Even from as far away as they were, the animals could see their boy-star was ruined. Skin hung off his face and arms in strips. His shirt was in tattered wet shreds at his waist. The boy's chest was burned open. Bones in his ribcage were visible. He was missing the hair from the front of his head.

As he stumbled closer, the shocked animals could see that his eyelids were gone and his wide blue eyes darted back and forth as he howled in agony through his melted lips.

Another rumbling sound came from the mound.

The surviving animals went berserk in the steaming aftermath of the geyser's eruption—especially with the prospect of another coming. They turned away from the mound of mud and fled.

Mark dropped his camera at his feet and flew over the trees toward the bus. The bats followed.

The Fumigator sprayed her scent across Happy's chest in panic as she ran and rammed herself into a snapped-off tree branch. It went straight through her eye and into her little skunk brain. She died shooting her stinky juice in an arc during her death spasm. It squirted into Happy's eyes as he turned from the horrifying scene and fled.

The burning-eyed bear charged through the forest, bouncing around like a huge stinky pinball. He finally made it out of the trees and ran straight into the bus that Mark was driving crazily down the secret road. Mark crashed the bus into the trees, pinning the bear between the bus and an ancient white pine. The bird got out and walked around to the front of the bus to investigate.

The angry bear was crushed.

With his dying breath, Happy said, "Fucking skunk blinded me with her stink juice."

Since the bus was still running, Mark dug around until he found a siphoning hose in the luggage compartment. He attached it to the exhaust pipe and fed it into the vent for the restroom. He'd convinced the bats to hide in there, and he'd locked them all in.

Mark had to smash a few bats who tried to wiggle out of the vent, but their bodies made it easier to stuff the vent closed and tape it shut. The rest of the bats went to sleep and never woke up. Which is an okay way for a bat to die. Except for being in the bus restroom. You shouldn't wish that sort of death on your worst enemy, really.

With the bats dead or dying, Mark flew back to the geyser.

He found Cage sitting beside a rat he knew only by reputation and a Steller's Jay he knew too well. The boy was stripping latex makeup off his face.

"It stinks around here," Mark said upon landing.

"What a bitch, huh?" said Dirty Bird, hooking a wing toward the skewered skunk.

"You said it." Mark hugged his cousin.

The egret turned to Cage. "I'm sorry for what we put you through. I was on your side all along, thanks to my cousin Dirty and his mad texting skills." He held up his phone.

Cage smiled, tossing latex into a bag. He pulled on his dry shirt. "Thank you, Mark," he answered. "And thank you, Dirty Bird. And you, Julio, thank you for your pyrotechnics. And for saving me. It made me feel good to know you trusted me when I found that note."

The rat looked up at the kid and smiled, "Technically that was *hydrotechnics*. Would have been even better if we'd had more time to set up, but the bear kept his mouth shut about the exact location 'til nearly too late. It was a bitch heating all that water on time—not to mention rounding up all those fucking ground squirrels. Aw, you're welcome, kid. Of course I trust you. I told you the biggest secret on Earth, and you kept it. You are a rare animal, Cage. And now you're an actor."

Dirty Bird bounced on one foot, "Don't forget the dead ground squirrel puppet show! I play a pretty mean ground squirrel!"

Mark looked around at the dead animals littering the clearing. "What are we going to do now?" he asked.

Dirty Bird looked at Julio and Cage. "Well, first things first. Martini party!" He put a wing around the rat and one around the egret's leg.

The jay cocked his head at Cage, "At my new nearby cabin, of course. Don't worry Cage, the closest animals are pirates, hermits and religious nuts. None of them will have ever even heard of you. We'll live the simple life. For a while, anyway."

Cage asked, "But what about the bus? Won't there be an investigation? Won't the police come looking for us?"

"We're all dead!" answered Dirty. "I've been dead since you and your dad shot up the Opera House—there were so many bodies in there, a third of them were never identified. They went by invitations and who turned up missing. Julio was declared dead after the zombie massacre, because Stinkin' didn't want to admit that he'd left. Mark just died in a geyser accident with you and the rest of the crew."

Mark added, "Let me go unhook the asphyxiation tube from out of the bathroom vent and they'll blame Steven for smashing the bus into the bear and locking the bats in the bathroom—his little overdosed body is somewhere in there. Be right back." He flew off.

The two animals and the boy stood in silence for a few minutes. Dirty Bird pulled his flask out from under his wing and passed it to Julio.

Julio took a drink and said, "I'm really glad I came back." He passed the flask to Cage.

Dirty Bird nodded.

"Me, too. But where are our bodies?" the boy asked, taking a pull from the flask.

Dirty took the flask and tucked it back under his wing. "This is Yellowstone, Cage. There's wolves, coyotes, eagles, ravens, bears, bigfoot—you name it. Your bodies are eaten. Now follow us, walkers!" Dirty flew into the sky.

Mark joined him, rising from the ruins of the bus.

Cage made his way through the forest toward Dirty Bird's secret cabin with Julio at his side—following the birds to his first animal martini party.

THE END

ABOUT THE AUTHOR

Kevin Shamel is a New Bizarro Author. When he's not locked away writing, he's busy making zombie-cat puppets, sage tea, and throwing martini parties. His family is a constant source of love, angst, comedy, joy and insanity—perfect inspiration for writing Bizarro stories.

Visit his website: http://www.shamelesscreations. com for links to more writing and to see what's going on in his world.

Bizarro books

CATALOG   SPRING 2011

Bizarro Books publishes under the following imprints:

www.rawdogscreamingpress.com

www.eraserheadpress.com

www.afterbirthbooks.com

www.swallowdownpress.com

For all your Bizarro needs visit:

WWW.BIZARROCENTRAL.COM

Introduce yourselves to the bizarro genre and all of its authors with the Bizarro Starter Kit series. Each volume features short novels and short stories by ten of the leading bizarro authors, designed to give you a perfect sampling of the genre for only $5 plus shipping.

BB-0X1
"The Bizarro Starter Kit"
(Orange)

Featuring D. Harlan Wilson, Carlton Mellick III, Jeremy Robert Johnson, Kevin L Donihe, Gina Ranalli, Andre Duza, Vincent W. Sakowski, Steve Beard, John Edward Lawson, and Bruce Taylor.

236 pages $5

BB-0X2
"The Bizarro Starter Kit"
(Blue)

Featuring Ray Fracalossy, Jeremy C. Shipp, Jordan Krall, Mykle Hansen, Andersen Prunty, Eckhard Gerdes, Bradley Sands, Steve Aylett, Christian TeBordo, and Tony Rauch.

244 pages $5

BB-001 "The Kafka Effekt" D. Harlan Wilson - A collection of forty-four irreal short stories loosely written in the vein of Franz Kafka, with more than a pinch of William S. Burroughs sprinkled on top. **211 pages** **$14**

BB-002 "Satan Burger" Carlton Mellick III - The cult novel that put Carlton Mellick III on the map ... Six punks get jobs at a fast food restaurant owned by the devil in a city violently overpopulated by surreal alien cultures. **236 pages** **$14**

BB-003 "Some Things Are Better Left Unplugged" Vincent Sakwoski - Join The Man and his Nemesis, the obese tabby, for a nightmare roller coaster ride into this postmodern fantasy. **152 pages** **$10**

BB-004 "Shall We Gather At the Garden?" Kevin L Donihe - Donihe's Debut novel. Midgets take over the world, The Church of Lionel Richie vs. The Church of the Byrds, plant porn and more! **244 pages** **$14**

BB-005 "Razor Wire Pubic Hair" Carlton Mellick III - A genderless humandildo is purchased by a razor dominatrix and brought into her nightmarish world of bizarre sex and mutilation. **176 pages** **$11**

BB-006 "Stranger on the Loose" D. Harlan Wilson - The fiction of Wilson's 2nd collection is planted in the soil of normalcy, but what grows out of that soil is a dark, witty, otherworldly jungle... **228 pages** **$14**

BB-007 "The Baby Jesus Butt Plug" Carlton Mellick III - Using clones of the Baby Jesus for anal sex will be the hip sex fetish of the future. **92 pages** **$10**

BB-008 "Fishyfleshed" Carlton Mellick III - The world of the past is an illogical flatland lacking in dimension and color, a sick-scape of crispy squid people wandering the desert for no apparent reason. **260 pages** **$14**

BB-009 **"Dead Bitch Army" Andre Duza** - Step into a world filled with racist teenagers, cannibals, 100 warped Uncle Sams, automobiles with razor-sharp teeth, living graffiti, and a pissed-off zombie bitch out for revenge. **344 pages $16**

BB-010 **"The Menstruating Mall" Carlton Mellick III** - "The Breakfast Club meets Chopping Mall as directed by David Lynch." - Brian Keene **212 pages $12**

BB-011 **"Angel Dust Apocalypse" Jeremy Robert Johnson** - Meth-heads, man-made monsters, and murderous Neo-Nazis. "Seriously amazing short stories..." - Chuck Palahniuk, author of Fight Club **184 pages $11**

BB-012 **"Ocean of Lard" Kevin L Donihe / Carlton Mellick III** - A parody of those old Choose Your Own Adventure kid's books about some very odd pirates sailing on a sea made of animal fat. **176 pages $12**

BB-013 **"Last Burn in Hell" John Edward Lawson** - From his lurid angst-affair with a lesbian music diva to his ascendance as unlikely pop icon the one constant for Kenrick Brimley, official state prison gigolo, is he's got no clue what he's doing. **172 pages $14**

BB-014 **"Tangerinephant" Kevin Dole 2** - TV-obsessed aliens have abducted Michael Tangerinephant in this bizarro combination of science fiction, satire, and surrealism. **164 pages $11**

BB-015 **"Foop!" Chris Genoa** - Strange happenings are going on at Dactyl, Inc, the world's first and only time travel tourism company.

"A surreal pie in the face!" - Christopher Moore **300 pages $14**

BB-016 **"Spider Pie" Alyssa Sturgill** - A one-way trip down a rabbit hole inhabited by sexual deviants and friendly monsters, fairytale beginnings and hideous endings. **104 pages $11**

BB-017 "The Unauthorized Woman" Efrem Emerson - Enter the world of the inner freak, a landscape populated by the pre-dead and morticioners, by cockroaches and 300-lb robots. **104 pages $11**

BB-018 "Fugue XXIX" Forrest Aguirre - Tales from the fringe of speculative literary fiction where innovative minds dream up the future's uncharted territories while mining forgotten treasures of the past. **220 pages $16**

BB-019 "Pocket Full of Loose Razorblades" John Edward Lawson - A collection of dark bizarro stories. From a giant rectum to a foot-fungus factory to a girl with a biforked tongue. **190 pages $13**

BB-020 "Punk Land" Carlton Mellick III - In the punk version of Heaven, the anarchist utopia is threatened by corporate fascism and only Goblin, Mortician's sperm, and a blue-mohawked female assassin named Shark Girl can stop them. **284 pages $15**

BB-021 "Pseudo-City" D. Harlan Wilson - Pseudo-City exposes what waits in the bathroom stall, under the manhole cover and in the corporate boardroom, all in a way that can only be described as mind-bogglingly irreal. **220 pages $16**

BB-022 "Kafka's Uncle and Other Strange Tales" Bruce Taylor - Anslenot and his giant tarantula (tormentor? fri-end?) wander a desecrated world in this novel and collection of stories from Mr. Magic Realism Himself. **348 pages $17**

BB-023 "Sex and Death In Television Town" Carlton Mellick III - In the old west, a gang of hermaphrodite gunslingers take refuge from a demon plague in Telos: a town where its citizens have televisions instead of heads. **184 pages $12**

BB-024 "It Came From Below The Belt" Bradley Sands - What can Grover Goldstein do when his severed, sentient penis forces him to return to high school and help it win the presidential election? **204 pages $13**

BB-025 "Sick: An Anthology of Illness" John Lawson, editor - These Sick stories are horrendous and hilarious dissections of creative minds on the scalpel's edge. **296 pages $16**

BB-026 "Tempting Disaster" John Lawson, editor - A shocking and alluring anthology from the fringe that examines our culture's obsession with taboos. **260 pages $16**

BB-027 "Siren Promised" Jeremy Robert Johnson - Nominated for the Bram Stoker Award. A potent mix of bad drugs, bad dreams, brutal bad guys, and surreal/incredible art by Alan M. Clark. **190 pages $13**

BB-028 "Chemical Gardens" Gina Ranalli - Ro and punk band Green is the Enemy find Kreepkins, a surfer-dude warlock, a vengeful demon, and a Metal Priestess in their way as they try to escape an underground nightmare. **188 pages $13**

BB-029 "Jesus Freaks" Andre Duza - For God so loved the world that he gave his only two begotten sons… and a few million zombies. **400 pages $16**

BB-030 "Grape City" Kevin L. Donihe - More Donihe-style comedic bizarro about a demon named Charles who is forced to work a minimum wage job on Earth after Hell goes out of business. **108 pages $10**

BB-031"Sea of the Patchwork Cats" Carlton Mellick III - A quiet dreamlike tale set in the ashes of the human race. For Mellick enthusiasts who also adore The Twilight Zone. **112 pages $10**

BB-032 "Extinction Journals" Jeremy Robert Johnson - An uncanny voyage across a newly nuclear America where one man must confront the problems associated with loneliness, insane dieties, radiation, love, and an ever-evolving cockroach suit with a mind of its own. **104 pages $10**

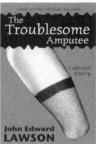

BB-033 **"Meat Puppet Cabaret" Steve Beard** - At last! The secret connection between Jack the Ripper and Princess Diana's death revealed! **240 pages $16 / $30**

BB-034 **"The Greatest Fucking Moment in Sports" Kevin L. Donihe** - In the tradition of the surreal anti-sitcom Get A Life comes a tale of triumph and agape love from the master of comedic bizarro. **108 pages $10**

BB-035 **"The Troublesome Amputee" John Edward Lawson** - Disturbing verse from a man who truly believes nothing is sacred and intends to prove it. **104 pages $9**

BB-036 **"Deity" Vic Mudd** - God (who doesn't like to be called "God") comes down to a typical, suburban, Ohio family for a little vacation—but it doesn't turn out to be as relaxing as He had hoped it would be… **168 pages $12**

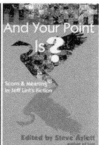

BB-037 **"The Haunted Vagina" Carlton Mellick III** - It's difficult to love a woman whose vagina is a gateway to the world of the dead. **132 pages $10**

BB-038 **"Tales from the Vinegar Wasteland" Ray Fracalossy** - Witness: a man is slowly losing his face, a neighbor who periodically screams out for no apparent reason, and a house with a room that doesn't actually exist. **240 pages $14**

BB-039 **"Suicide Girls in the Afterlife" Gina Ranalli** - After Pogue commits suicide, she unexpectedly finds herself an unwilling "guest" at a hotel in the Afterlife, where she meets a group of bizarre characters, including a goth Satan, a hippie Jesus, and an alien-human hybrid. **100 pages $9**

BB-040 **"And Your Point Is?" Steve Aylett** - In this follow-up to LINT multiple authors provide critical commentary and essays about Jeff Lint's mind-bending literature. **104 pages $11**

BB-041 **"Not Quite One of the Boys" Vincent Sakowski** - While drug-dealer Maxi drinks with Dante in purgatory, God and Satan play a little tri-level chess and do a little bargaining over his business partner, Vinnie, who is still left on earth. **220 pages $14**

BB-042 **"Teeth and Tongue Landscape" Carlton Mellick III** - On a planet made out of meat, a socially-obsessive monophobic man tries to find his place amongst the strange creatures and communities that he comes across. **110 pages $10**

BB-043 **"War Slut" Carlton Mellick III** - Part "1984," part "Waiting for Godot," and part action horror video game adaptation of John Carpenter's "The Thing." **116 pages $10**

BB-044 **"All Encompassing Trip" Nicole Del Sesto** - In a world where coffee is no longer available, the only television shows are reality TV re-runs, and the animals are talking back, Nikki, Amber and a singing Coyote in a do-rag are out to restore the light **308 pages $15**

BB-045 **"Dr. Identity" D. Harlan Wilson** - Follow the Dystopian Duo on a killing spree of epic proportions through the irreal postcapitalist city of Bliptown where time ticks sideways, artificial Bug-Eyed Monsters punish citizens for consumer-capitalist lethargy, and ultraviolence is as essential as a daily multivitamin. **208 pages $15**

BB-046 **"The Million-Year Centipede" Eckhard Gerdes** - Wakelin, frontman for 'The Hinge,' wrote a poem so prophetic that to ignore it dooms a person to drown in blood. **130 pages $12**

BB-047 **"Sausagey Santa" Carlton Mellick III** - A bizarro Christmas tale featuring Santa as a piratey mutant with a body made of sausages. 124 pages $10

BB-048 **"Misadventures in a Thumbnail Universe" Vincent Sakowski** - Dive deep into the surreal and satirical realms of neo-classical Blender Fiction, filled with television shoes and flesh-filled skies. **120 pages $10**

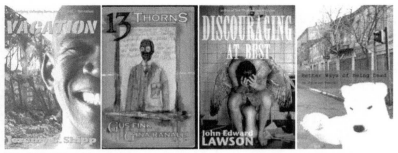

BB-049 **"Vacation" Jeremy C. Shipp** - Blueblood Bernard Johnson leaves his boring life behind to go on The Vacation, a year-long corporate sponsored odyssey. But instead of seeing the world, Bernard is captured by terrorists, becomes a key figure in secret drug wars, and, worse, doesn't once miss his secure American Dream. **160 pages $14**

BB-051 **"13 Thorns" Gina Ranalli** - Thirteen tales of twisted, bizarro horror. **240 pages $13**

BB-050 **"Discouraging at Best" John Edward Lawson** - A collection where the absurdity of the mundane expands exponentially creating a tidal wave that sweeps reason away. For those who enjoy satire, bizarro, or a good old-fashioned slap to the senses. **208 pages $15**

BB-052 **"Better Ways of Being Dead" Christian TeBordo** - In this class, the students have to keep one palm down on the table at all times, and listen to lectures about a panda who speaks Chinese. **216 pages $14**

BB-053 **"Ballad of a Slow Poisoner" Andrew Goldfarb** Millford Mutterwurst sat down on a Tuesday to take his afternoon tea, and made the unpleasant discovery that his elbows were becoming flatter. **128 pages $10**

BB-054 **"Wall of Kiss" Gina Ranalli** - A woman... A wall... Sometimes love blooms in the strangest of places. **108 pages $9**

BB-055 **"HELP! A Bear is Eating Me" Mykle Hansen** - The bizarro, heartwarming, magical tale of poor planning, hubris and severe blood loss... **150 pages $11**

BB-056 **"Piecemeal June" Jordan Krall** - A man falls in love with a living sex doll, but with love comes danger when her creator comes after her with crab-squid assassins. **90 pages $9**

BB-057 **"Laredo" Tony Rauch** - Dreamlike, surreal stories by Tony Rauch. **180 pages $12**

BB-058 **"The Overwhelming Urge" Andersen Prunty** - A collection of bizarro tales by Andersen Prunty. **150 pages $11**

BB-059 **"Adolf in Wonderland" Carlton Mellick III** - A dreamlike adventure that takes a young descendant of Adolf Hitler's design and sends him down the rabbit hole into a world of imperfection and disorder. **180 pages $11**

BB-060 **"Super Cell Anemia" Duncan B. Barlow** - "Unrelentingly bizarre and mysterious, unsettling in all the right ways..." - Brian Evenson. **180 pages $12**

BB-061 **"Ultra Fuckers" Carlton Mellick III** - Absurdist suburban horror about a couple who enter an upper middle class gated community but can't find their way out. **108 pages $9**

BB-062 **"House of Houses" Kevin L. Donihe** - An odd man wants to marry his house. Unfortunately, all of the houses in the world collapse at the same time in the Great House Holocaust. Now he must travel to House Heaven to find his departed fiancee. **172 pages $11**

BB-063 **"Necro Sex Machine" Andre Duza** - The Dead Bicth returns in this follow-up to the bizarro zombie epic Dead Bitch Army. **400 pages $16**

BB-064 **"Squid Pulp Blues" Jordan Krall** - In these three bizarro-noir novellas, the reader is thrown into a world of murderers, drugs made from squid parts, deformed gun-toting veterans, and a mischievous apocalyptic donkey. **204 pages $12**

BB-065 **"Jack and Mr. Grin" Andersen Prunty** - "When Mr. Grin calls you can hear a smile in his voice. Not a warm and friendly smile, but the kind that seizes your spine in fear. You don't need to pay your phone bill to hear it. That smile is in every line of Prunty's prose." - Tom Bradley. **208 pages $12**

BB-066 **"Cybernetrix" Carlton Mellick III** - What would you do if your normal everyday world was slowly mutating into the video game world from Tron? **212 pages $12**

BB-067 **"Lemur" Tom Bradley** - Spencer Sproul is a would-be serial-killing bus boy who can't manage to murder, injure, or even scare anybody. However, there are other ways to do damage to far more people and do it legally... **120 pages $12**

BB-068 **"Cocoon of Terror" Jason Earls** - Decapitated corpses...a sculpture of terror...Zelian's masterpiece, his Cocoon of Terror, will trigger a supernatural disaster for everyone on Earth. **196 pages $14**

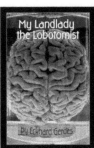

BB-069 **"Mother Puncher" Gina Ranalli** - The world has become tragically over-populated and now the government strongly opposes procreation. Ed is employed by the government as a mother-puncher. He doesn't relish his job, but he knows it has to be done and he knows he's the best one to do it. **120 pages $9**

BB-070 **"My Landlady the Lobotomist" Eckhard Gerdes** - The brains of past tenants line the shelves of my boarding house, soaking in a mysterious elixir. One more slip-up and the landlady might just add my frontal lobe to her collection. **116 pages $12**

BB-071 **"CPR for Dummies" Mickey Z.** - This hilarious freakshow at the world's end is the fragmented, sobering debut novel by acclaimed nonfiction author Mickey Z. **216 pages $14**

BB-072 **"Zerostrata" Andersen Prunty** - Hansel Nothing lives in a tree house, suffers from memory loss, has a very eccentric family, and falls in love with a woman who runs naked through the woods every night. **144 pages $11**

BB-073 **"The Egg Man" Carlton Mellick III** - It is a world where humans reproduce like insects. Children are the property of corporations, and having an enormous ten-foot brain implanted into your skull is a grotesque sexual fetish. Mellick's industrial urban dystopia is one of his darkest and grittiest to date. **184 pages $11**

BB-074 **"Shark Hunting in Paradise Garden" Cameron Pierce** - A group of strange humanoid religious fanatics travel back in time to the Garden of Eden to discover it is invested with hundreds of giant flying maneating sharks. **150 pages $10**

BB-075 **"Apeshit" Carlton Mellick III** - Friday the 13th meets Visitor Q. Six hipster teens go to a cabin in the woods inhabited by a deformed killer. An incredibly fucked-up parody of B-horror movies with a bizarro slant. **192 pages $12**

BB-076 **"Rampaging Fuckers of Everything on the Crazy Shitting Planet of the Vomit At smosphere" Mykle Hansen** - 3 bizarro satires. Monster Cocks, Journey to the Center of Agnes Cuddlebottom, and Crazy Shitting Planet. **228 pages $12**

BB-077 **"The Kissing Bug" Daniel Scott Buck** - In the tradition of Roald Dahl, Tim Burton, and Edward Gorey, comes this bizarro anti-war children's story about a bohemian conenose kissing bug who falls in love with a human woman. **116 pages $10**

BB-078 **"MachoPoni" Lotus Rose** - It's My Little Pony... *Bizarro* style! A long time ago Poniworld was split in two. On one side of the Jagged Line is the Pastel Kingdom, a magical land of music, parties, and positivity. On the other side of the Jagged Line is Dark Kingdom inhabited by an army of undead ponies. **148 pages $11**

BB-079 **"The Faggiest Vampire" Carlton Mellick III** - A Roald Dahl-esque children's story about two faggy vampires who partake in a mustache competition to find out which one is truly the faggiest. **104 pages $10**

BB-080 **"Sky Tongues" Gina Ranalli** - The autobiography of Sky Tongues, the biracial hermaphrodite actress with tongues for fingers. Follow her strange life story as she rises from freak to fame. **204 pages $12**

BB-081 **"Washer Mouth" Kevin L. Donihe** - A washing machine becomes human and pursues his dream of meeting his favorite soap opera star. **244 pages $11**

BB-082 **"Shatnerquake" Jeff Burk** - All of the characters ever played by William Shatner are suddenly sucked into our world. Their mission: hunt down and destroy the real William Shatner. **100 pages $10**

BB-083 **"The Cannibals of Candyland" Carlton Mellick III** - There exists a race of cannibals that are made of candy. They live in an underground world made out of candy. One man has dedicated his life to killing them all. **170 pages $11**

BB-084 **"Slub Glub in the Weird World of the Weeping Willows" Andrew Goldfarb** - The charming tale of a blue glob named Slub Glub who helps the weeping willows whose tears are flooding the earth. There are also hyenas, ghosts, and a voodoo priest **100 pages $10**

COMING SOON

"Fistful of Feet" by Jordan Krall
"Ass Goblins of Auschwitz" by Cameron Pierce
"Cursed" by Jeremy C. Shipp
"Warrior Wolf Women of the Wasteland"
by Carlton Mellick III
"The Kobold Wizard's Dildo of Enlightenment +2"
by Carlton Mellick III

ORDER FORM

TITLES	QTY	PRICE	TOTAL

Please make checks and moneyorders payable to ROSE O'KEEFE / BIZARRO BOOKS in U.S. funds only. Please don't send bad checks! Allow 2-6 weeks for delivery. International orders may take longer. If you'd like to pay online via PAYPAL.COM, send payments to publisher@eraserheadpress.com.

SHIPPING: US ORDERS - $2 for the first book, $1 for each additional book. For priority shipping, add an additional $4. INT'L ORDERS - $5 for the first book, $3 for each additional book. Add an additional $5 per book for global priority shipping.

Send payment to:

BIZARRO BOOKS
 C/O Rose O'Keefe
 205 NE Bryant
 Portland, OR 97211

Address

City   State   Zip

Email   Phone

Lightning Source UK Ltd.
Milton Keynes UK
UKHW011010180123
415553UK00001B/142